Disney

CHiLLS

FiENDS ON THE OTHER SIDE

Disney CHILLS

FIENDS ON THE OTHER SIDE

By Vera Strange

Disney PRESS

Los Angeles · New York

Printed in the United States of America
First Paperback Edition, October 2020
5 7 9 10 8 6 4
FAC-025438-21092

Library of Congress Control Number: 2020930926
ISBN 978-1-368-04836-1

For more Disney Press fun, visit www.disneybooks.com

SUSTAINABLE
FORESTRY
INITIATIVE

Certified Sourcing

www.sfiprogram.org
SFI-01054

The SFI label applies to the text stock

The dreams that you
FEAR will come true.

1

IN THE SHADOWS

"**W**ho can tell me what causes a *shadow*?" Mrs. Perkins said, jabbing her index finger at the image of the sun projected on the screen.

Jamal squinted from the back of the class. His teacher wore a hideous floral-print dress the color of goopy pink stomach medicine that matched the slight sunburn on her normally milky-white arms. Her perfectly round face was accented by a pair of perfectly round glasses with thick lenses that made her look like an owl. Or at least, that was what Jamal had always thought.

Her huge green eyes scanned the class expectantly. Jamal thrust his hand up. *I know the answer,* he thought. *Pick me!* He loved science class the most. Science felt like a never-ending puzzle he could try to solve. Even better, the more he learned, the more exciting it got.

But Mrs. Perkins's oversized eyes looked right over him—and her gaze landed on his brother. His *twin* brother. Identical twin, to be exact. Malik was technically older than Jamal, having been born a full five minutes earlier.

And he never let Jamal forget it.

"*Malik*," Mrs. Perkins said, calling on Jamal's brother instead. Like Jamal didn't even exist. Like he was invisible.

"Right, a shadow is caused by an object blocking the rays of the sun," Malik said, oblivious to his brother's sullen expression. "The bigger the object, the bigger the shadow."

"Correct, as always." Mrs. Perkins beamed at Malik, which made her eyes appear even larger. "No wonder you're the top student in my class. Heck, the whole school."

"You know it, Mrs. P," Malik said with a cocky grin and a wink. "Straight As all the way."

If Jamal called a teacher by a casual nickname like that, he'd probably be reprimanded, maybe even sent to the principal's office. But not Malik. He was both the smartest *and* the most popular kid at Princess River Middle School, which meant he could get away with anything. If Jamal ever got noticed—a rare occurrence—it was never for something good. There was, for instance, the horrific gym wedgie incident of last year, a memory that made Jamal squirm. It involved a big kid named Colton, who always picked on Jamal and who had, apparently, recently perfected his wedgie-giving skills. Suffice it to say, Jamal hadn't worn tighty-whities to school since. But aside from that nightmare, most of the time it was like he didn't exist.

While Mrs. Perkins blathered on about the sun's rays, Jamal studied his brother's face—high cheekbones, freckled brown skin, mop of curly black hair that made him a few inches taller. It was like staring at his own reflection. How could they be the same in so many ways—birthday, age, appearance, parents—yet so different at the same time?

Maybe Jamal *wasn't* invisible. Maybe he was a shadow—there, but unnoticed—and his brother, Malik, was the large object blocking the rays of the sun.

FIENDS ON THE OTHER SIDE

Knock. Knock. Knock.

There was a tentative rap on the door.

Jamal jerked his eyes away from his brother. "Come on in," Mrs. Perkins said in a singsong voice.

The door swung open to reveal a girl whom Jamal had never seen before. She had brown skin a touch lighter than Jamal's and wore punk skater clothes—skinny jeans torn at the knees, paired with a fluorescent logo shirt and scuffed black-and-white Vans. He could tell that she was a *real* skater from her scabby knees and skinned elbows. Her hair was shaved into a short Mohawk and dyed bright purple.

This girl stood out.

Jamal couldn't stop staring at her.

"Uh, I think this is my class. I'm Riley . . . DeSeroux. I just transferred to Princess River." She thrust out a crumpled class schedule, casting her gaze down to her feet.

"Welcome to science class, Ms. DeSeroux," Mrs. Perkins said, studying the paper through her oversized glasses. "Go ahead and take a seat."

Riley slid into the empty seat next to Jamal. It was empty for a reason. Nobody wanted to sit next to Jamal.

Except the new girl.

She'll wise up soon, he thought glumly. It's not that he didn't want to make a new friend. Well, a friend . . . *period*.

Jamal didn't really have any friends. The closest thing was Malik, but brothers didn't count. They had to hang out with you, at least sometimes. After all, he and Malik shared a small bedroom and a set of parental units. But these days, they didn't spend much time together. Malik was too busy with his fan club, as Jamal thought of his brother's popular friends, who all seemed to worship the ground he walked on.

Jamal glanced at Riley again. He knew it was bad to stare at the sun, but he couldn't help it. She practically glowed. But that could have been her bright shirt.

He considered whispering something like "Hey, welcome to Princess River." Or maybe "Want me to show you around campus?"

But it sounded silly even in his head. Still, he tried to muster up the courage. He cleared his throat.

"Hey, Riley—" he started.

The bell rang, cutting him off. The class bolted up and crowded around Malik, rushing into the hall. Jamal was left alone, plodding toward the door. Even Riley sped away, leaving him in her dust. He watched her back as she disappeared into the crowded hallway packed with rowdy students.

It was for the better anyway. Even if Jamal had been able to introduce himself, Riley would have forgotten he existed as soon as she met Malik. That's what always happened. It wasn't worth trying to talk to her. He had always felt invisible, but after Mrs. Perkins's lecture, he realized he was more like a shadow. His outline was there, but nobody paid attention to him, especially not when he was standing next to his brother.

That was how it had always been.

"And that's how it'll always be," he muttered with a sigh. He trudged toward his locker and saw Malik nearby, surrounded by his fan club. Envy rose in Jamal's heart. It burned but also felt somehow comforting: he was so used to feeling this way. He opened his locker and rooted around for the books he'd need for the next few classes, listening to Malik's friends laugh at his jokes.

Suddenly, a voice startled him.

"So, what superpower do you wish you had?"

Jamal jerked his gaze away from his brother to find Riley standing right next to him. She swung her backpack, bulging with fresh books, over her shoulder.

"Would you rather have invisibility powers," she continued with a smirk, "or be able to fly?"

Jamal glanced behind him, convinced that she must be talking to somebody else. But nobody was there. It was just the two of them. And her eyes were fixed on *him*.

"Uh, what?" Jamal said, confused both by the fact that she was actually talking to him and by her strange question.

"You know, the old superhero conundrum," she said, pointing to his shirt. The one with his favorite comic book hero on it. He glanced down at it, and his cheeks burned.

"Oh, right," he said, mentally searching for something cool to say. Though the truth was he didn't even have to think about it. He already knew the answer. "Obviously, I want to be able to fly."

She frowned. "Oh, and why's that?"

"That way everybody would notice me."

Riley gave him a strange look. "You know, invisibility

is the stronger superpower. Most people choose that one."

"Not in my world," Jamal said, slamming his locker shut with a deep sigh. "I already have invisibility powers. And trust me, they're not *super*."

He hurried off down the hall to his next class, leaving her standing in his shadow.

* * *

"Fine, we'll take . . . *Jamal*," Colton said with disgust, like he'd just been told he had to kiss a slimy frog, not pick a basketball teammate in gym class. Colton had moved to New Orleans from Texas a couple of years back and reminded Jamal of a stereotypical cowboy—tall and always tan, with shaggy blond hair and a square jaw. If he'd been cast in an old Western movie, he would have been the villain, for sure. "Not like we have a choice."

Gym class was turning out to be even worse than science class. Despite his best efforts to stand tall and look strong, Jamal got picked last. Of course, his brother got picked first for the opposing team. He was the best player at Princess River Middle, and everyone knew it.

They were identical twins. They should have been *equally* good at basketball, but for some reason, Jamal lacked the athletic coordination and skill that came so easily to his brother.

It just wasn't fair.

Even so, he ran up and down the court. He hustled for every pass, but it felt like his hands were made of lead. His fingers couldn't grip the ball. His dribble was terrible. All his shots were air balls. Meanwhile, Malik blocked shots at one end and swished the ball through the net like the opening was five feet across. He simply couldn't miss. He made it look effortless.

Worse yet, Riley had a pass to get out of gym class, so she sat in the bleachers, scribbling in a black-and-white composition notebook. Jamal kept catching her glancing over at his horrific performance on the court. He already felt a little bit guilty for blowing her off in the hall earlier, but this just made it worse. He desperately wanted to talk to her and impress her. More than anything, he wished he could have an actual friend. One who wasn't related to him. But if she hadn't already thought he was a loser, he decided, then she certainly would now.

What else could possibly go wrong today?

That's when the buzzer sounded, signaling the end of the game, and he looked at the scoreboard. His team had lost 58 to 23. Jamal hadn't even managed to score one point, while his brother had scored the most points on the winning team.

Jamal watched Malik's teammates cheer for his brother. "You schooled them!"

They surrounded Malik and paraded triumphantly toward the locker room. Jamal's teammates were silent, glaring at him.

"We only lost because of you," Colton muttered. "You missed every shot. Your brother ran all over you."

Another kid from his team bumped him. Jamal stumbled into the bleachers. His shin thumped the edge. Pain shot through his leg. "H-hey, I'm sorry," he stammered. "I'll do better next time—"

"The way you played defense," Colton spat, towering over Jamal, "you may as well have been *invisible*."

"I swear . . . I tried my best," Jamal said. "Just gimme another chance—"

But Colton, his face twisted with anger, shoved Jamal into the bleachers.

Out of the corner of his eye, Jamal caught Riley watching them. She looked concerned. Jamal felt fiery blood rush to his cheeks, making them burn. His hopes of being her friend faded altogether. The rest of the kids from his team surrounded him and Colton.

"Whatcha gonna do now, Invisible Boy?" Colton sneered. The other kids jeered and laughed cruelly.

Jamal's mind flashed back to the horrific gym wedgie incident. This was going to be way worse, he could already tell. The furious expression on Colton's face told him that much. "No, please . . ." he begged. "I'm sorry! I'll play better—"

Then a shadow stretched over them. It was accompanied by a stern voice.

"Hey, leave him alone!"

2

INVISIBLE BOY

The shadow belonged to Malik.

"Stop messing with my brother," Malik said, glaring at Colton. "Don't you have something better to do?"

"Hey, it's chill," Colton said, throwing his hands up and backing away from Jamal. "We didn't mean anything by it. We were just having a little team chat, that's all—"

"Right, well don't let me catch you *chatting* with my brother again," Malik said. "Or you'll have to answer to me, got it?"

Colton looked down and blushed. His cheeks turned red beneath his freckles. Jamal couldn't believe it. Then Malik shifted his irate gaze to the other kids.

"That means . . . *all of you*. Buzz off and leave Jamal alone. Is that clear?"

They didn't need to be told twice. Colton and the rest of Jamal's team headed for the locker room, looking chastised. Once Malik was satisfied that they were gone, he held out his arm to help Jamal up. "You okay, Little J?"

That had been his nickname for Jamal ever since they were kids. At first, Jamal hadn't liked the name. "How am I the *little* one?" he would shoot back. "We're, like, the exact same age."

"No way, I'm older," Malik would say, puffing out his chest.

"Please, like a whole five minutes," Jamal would say, rolling his eyes.

"It still counts," Malik would reply with a smirk. Then they'd both laugh. That was their routine. But over time, the name had grown on him. Now he liked it when Malik called him that.

"Yeah, thanks," Jamal said, staggering to his feet and limping on his injured leg. He gritted his teeth.

He glanced over and caught Riley watching them from the bleachers. *Just great,* he thought with a grimace.

Now she's never gonna be my friend. His shin still hurt from banging it, but his ego hurt more. He burned with shame over needing his brother's help.

"But you know," he added, trying to look tough, "I had it all under control."

"Under control, huh?" Malik said, shaking his head. His gaze fixed on Jamal's injured leg. "Sure, you did."

Even though he sounded skeptical, he let it go.

"You know, I'm always here for you," Malik said, softening his tone. "I'm sorry I've been so busy this year. But I've always got your back."

"I know, me too," Jamal said, feeling even more ashamed. *Like Malik would ever need my help for anything.*

"Brothers *forever*," Malik said, holding out his fist. This was their little ritual, which had also started when they were kids.

"Brothers *forever*," Jamal repeated, bumping Malik's fist with his.

"That's more like it," Malik said with a grin. Jamal returned the grin, but it felt forced. Shame still burned his cheeks.

They headed for the locker room to shower. Jamal did

his best to hide his limp. He didn't want Malik to know how much he really had needed his help. He knew that his brother loved him. It went without saying. But it still bothered Jamal that he wasn't good enough on his own, that he had needed his brother's help in the first place.

Even worse, he had a sinking feeling that most of his problems were because of Malik. His brother was just too good . . . at *everything*. It didn't leave Jamal much room to get noticed.

He studied his brother's visage—so similar to his own—and wondered what it would be like to be him. To be the popular kid. To get called on in science class. To have actual friends. To get picked first in gym class.

What would that feel like?

* * *

After showering, they lined up in the gym to collect their school yearbooks. Excited chatter echoed through the room. Jamal waited his turn. His hands finally closed around the hardbound book. Excitement coursed through him.

He flipped it open, turning the glossy pages filled with

colorful photographs. Picture after picture showed Malik sinking shots on the basketball court, playing trumpet in the jazz band, leading the pep rally. Page after page, picture after picture, but Jamal didn't appear once. He even squinted at the backgrounds of the pictures, hoping to glimpse his face, even a blurry version. But *nothing*.

Then he flipped to the superlatives, but that was even worse. Malik had been voted everything.

Most Popular. Most Musical. Most Likely to Succeed. Best Athlete.

Jamal didn't get voted anything, of course. What made it worse was that he was *actually* good at a few things — or so he thought, even if nobody else seemed to notice. Science, for starters. His grades in Mrs. Perkins's class were all As. He also loved creative writing. When he wrote stories, he could be anything or travel anywhere. That was the only time he felt truly free and out of his brother's shadow. But none of those talents were highlighted in the yearbook's pages. *What does it matter being good at something if nobody notices?* he thought glumly.

Feeling even worse, Jamal flipped to the class photos. At least he was guaranteed a spot on one of those pages.

Every kid got a class picture. As always, his photo was right next to his brother's. They had the same last name and were in the same class.

His brother beamed with a confident smile in his school portrait, while Jamal's picture was . . . well . . . *horrid*.

Instead of a charming smile, his face was plastered with a lopsided frown. Even the image itself looked dark and blurry, like it was taken while he was in the middle of turning his head.

"Hey, Malik, sign my yearbook!"

Jamal glanced over to see his brother surrounded by his adoring fan club. They were all clamoring for him, their books open, offering their pens. Meanwhile, nobody was asking for Jamal's signature.

He slammed the book shut and hurried from the gym, not even bothering to ask anyone to sign his yearbook. He just couldn't deal with any more humiliation in one day.

* * *

Jamal hid outside the school until the buses pulled up. He watched as Malik and his fan club boarded the bus. He followed them like a shadow. He still clutched his year-book, though it really didn't feel like his at all. He was barely in it, unlike Malik.

Maybe Colton was right about him. Maybe he was Invisible Boy.

Still limping from the gym incident, he started to board the bus when the door began to shut.

"Hey, kid, watch out!"

A hand shot out and stopped the door before it could slam into his injured leg.

Jamal looked back—it was Riley. Her dark brown eyes were fixed on him, set off by her manic purple hair. He wanted to say something cool, something that would impress her and make this day less terrible. Malik would know just what to say. He had the ability to charm anyone.

But all words—cool or not—evaporated from his brain. It was like he'd lost the ability to speak. The silence grew longer and more awkward.

"Uh . . . thanks," was all he could muster before he darted up the steps and bolted for the back of the bus.

He slumped into the last row, feeling thoroughly humiliated. That was really the only word for it. He wanted so badly to talk to Riley. But every time he tried, it just made everything worse. He glanced around the bus, where all the other kids sat with their friends, goofing off and joking around. Jamal pulled up his hoodie and sank lower in his seat while the other kids chattered excitedly and signed each other's yearbooks.

May as well embrace my invisibility powers, he thought as the bus tore off, lurching over the pockmarked streets. The latest hurricane had left them scarred, and the city had yet to repave.

His eyes flipped to the sky. It was clear blue with only a few harmless clouds, but the weather could always turn in a city like New Orleans. This had always been his home, but that didn't make it an easy place to live. They had lost their previous house in a bad flood caused by the most recent big storm.

The bus made its way through the French Quarter. Jazz music drifted into the streets. Tourists stood in lines for famous beignets and Creole food. Tiana's, the best restaurant in town, had a line snaking out the doors and onto the sidewalk, as always.

A few minutes later, when the bus reached the edge

of the Quarter, a shop he'd never noticed before caught his eye. Oddly, it looked like it had been there a really long time. The sign read DR. FACILIER'S VOODOO EMPORIUM. Creepy dolls stared out from the shop's window. He shifted around to get a better view. They looked like handmade dolls, stitched together from crude burlap cloth. Their heads appeared lumpy and misshapen. Jamal had seen these types of dolls before, of course, but these were more horrid than most. There was something almost captivating about them. Somehow Jamal couldn't make himself look away.

And then the dolls looked at *him*.

His heart lurched. It couldn't be. But it was. Their eyes all locked on his face, moving to stay on him as the bus inched forward. What? How was that possible? They couldn't be—

Beep! Beep!

His phone went off in his pocket.

Jamal fumbled for it and hit silent, then jerked his head around to look back at the shop. But the Voodoo Emporium had passed out of sight, along with the odd dolls.

Probably just my imagination, he thought, though his heart was still pounding. Dolls couldn't move like that. But he couldn't shake the image of their eyes locking on to his face. To distract himself, he fished his phone out. His gaze landed on a new text message.

TO: *MALIK & JAMAL*

FROM: *MOM*

HOPE YOU HAD A GREAT DAY AT SCHOOL. YOU EACH RECEIVED A SPECIAL GIFT FROM YOUR GRANDMOTHER'S ESTATE. WE'LL OPEN THEM WHEN YOU GET HOME. LOVE & KISSES, MOM

Jamal had explained to his mother that she didn't need to sign her text messages—that he knew who was texting by the contact name on top. But like most adults, she wasn't very tech savvy.

He scanned the message again, feeling a shiver run up his spine. His grandmother had lived in one of those big old houses in the Garden District. She died just last month from a stroke, and they'd attended the funeral and wake. He could see her so clearly in his mind—black veils hiding her face and trailing long enough to cover her body, her gloved hands clutching a knobby cane.

Grandma had been allergic to sunlight and kept her whole body covered. He'd never even seen her face outside of the pictures the family had from before he was born. In those she was pretty, with dark skin already starting to wrinkle, and a wistful sort of smile. Now, she always kept herself hidden under veils. She also never left her house. According to his parents, his grandmother was a *recluse*.

As the bus barreled into their quaint little neighborhood on the outskirts of the city, heading for their house, Jamal stared at the text and another shiver rushed through him. He had never received a gift from a dead person before.

What could it be?

3

SPECIAL DELIVERY

The smell of gumbo hit Jamal's nostrils as soon as he stepped through the front door behind Malik. Rich, garlicky, spicy, meaty. It was unlike any other smell in the world. To Jamal, it smelled like home.

His mouth immediately started watering. Their dad, tall and broad-shouldered, with his hair freshly styled in perfect short twists, was stirring the contents of a big cast-iron pot on the stove with precision and loving care. That pot had been in their family for generations, same as their secret family gumbo recipe.

The screen door slammed shut behind him with a *thwap!*

Their mother looked up from a stack of bills on the

kitchen table, a colorful scarf tied around her hair to protect her dark curls, the way she always wore it on days she worked from home. "Go wash up, boys. Dinner will be ready soon."

The local news blared on the small television wedged onto the kitchen counter. "Hurricane Donald threatens New Orleans. . . . The category three storm is gaining strength as it barrels through the Gulf. . . . Could become a category five." Jamal's eyes locked on to the image of the distinctive cloud formation swirling over the ocean, tracking toward their city. He felt a tingle in his fingertips. That was so *strange*. He had just been thinking about the devastating storm that had destroyed his childhood home, and now another one was coming right for them.

Hurricanes had always fascinated him; they were another science puzzle he wanted to solve. They formed when warm, moist air from the ocean encountered cooler air. A hurricane was caused by the convergence of divergent forces that, when put together, could produce extreme devastation.

"Carter, turn that off," Mom said when she caught Jamal watching the screen. She dropped her voice. "We don't need to worry the kids. You know what we went through with that last storm. They've been through enough already."

She didn't need to lower her voice. Jamal *knew* what they had gone through. How could he forget? The water had rushed up from their basement, flooding the house. That was why they'd had to move to the outskirts of town. This house was farther from where their grandmother had lived in the Garden District, too. She'd died only a few short weeks after their move, before the city had even finished cleaning up from the storm. Jamal had always wondered if her stroke had something to do with the storm that had battered her beloved New Orleans.

Jamal followed Malik through the living room, where there was an old sofa and matching chairs, both a hideous shade of orange their mom considered stylish. The fireplace mantel was filled with family photographs. Jamal's gaze skimmed the familiar images. They all featured Malik doing something impressive—playing basketball, performing on trumpet in a concert, holding up a perfect report card. If Jamal was in the pictures at all, he was always in the background.

It was exactly like the yearbook. Just like everything else in his life. Malik stood out, while Jamal lurked in the shadows. He tore his eyes away from the family pictures, but not before he caught sight of a recent group photo of all his smiling cousins, aunts and uncles, and at the center was his grandmother, covered in black veils.

Jamal shuddered again. While most of his friends had warm, loving grandparents, his grandmother had been different. In fact, they had barely ever spoken. His mother always made excuses for her mom's odd behavior. "She's been through a lot. She prefers silence and darkness now."

But what had she been through, exactly? Why was she a recluse? Why did she refuse to leave her big, drafty house? Why did she hide under all those black veils, even when the sun wasn't out? What—or *whom*—was she hiding from?

But none of these questions had an answer. At least, not an answer he could get from his parents. His mom didn't like to talk about their grandmother.

He followed Malik into their bedroom. Two twin beds and matching dressers took up most of the room. Malik flopped onto his bed, covered with a superhero comforter, and flipped through his yearbook.

"You get any good ones?" he asked, holding the book open to a page filled with signatures from his fan club.

Jamal felt envy singe his heart, even though he knew it was wrong.

"Yeah, a whole bunch," he said, quickly stowing his yearbook in his dresser to hide the lie. "Uh, I'll show you later."

Malik had already defended him once that day. The last thing Jamal needed was more pity. His brother meant well, of course, but it only made everything worse. His eyes fell on the story he had written in English class the previous day, sitting on the dresser. It was about a prince kissing a frog and turning it into a princess, a twist on the old fairy tale. He called it *The Prince and the Frog*. He'd also changed the setting to New Orleans. He had always wanted his parents to read his writing, but he'd never been brave enough to show it to them. He took a deep breath and reached for the pages. Maybe he'd show the story to them after dinner.

"Kids, dinnertime!"

Their father's voice echoed through the small house. Their last house had been bigger, and Jamal had had his own bedroom. But he secretly preferred sharing a room with Malik, even though it meant less space. He didn't say it often, but he loved his brother, and he hated that he felt dark feelings about him sometimes. He did his best to keep them stuffed down in his heart, but they always had a way of spilling out stronger than before.

"Did you hear your father?" their mother called. "Dinner's getting cold."

That was their second warning. And it came from Mom. That meant they needed to get in there. *Now.*

"Hey, let's go eat," Jamal said, then grinned. "If you can tear yourself away from all those autographs."

Malik chuckled. "Well, I still don't have the most important one." He pointed to a blank corner. "I saved you a prime spot. You'd better sign it."

* * *

After helping their father do the dishes, including scrubbing the stubborn residue from the gumbo pot, their mother set two wooden boxes on the kitchen table in front of Jamal and Malik. "These are the special gifts your grandmother left for you."

Jamal studied the boxes, feeling a rush of anticipation despite his earlier fears. The box in front of Malik was larger and longer. Its polished wood surface was carved with the image of an alligator playing a trumpet.

But his box was different. It was smallish—about four inches by four inches. The wooden surface was also carved, but not with a cheerful image like his brother's box. Instead, a creepy skull stared back at him. The eye sockets were gouged out, as if with a crude tool, leaving deep scratch marks. He felt his pulse skip.

What did the images mean?

"Look, I know your grandmother could be a bit . . . strange," their mother said, struggling for words. Their father walked over and placed his hand on her shoulder in a show of support.

"The old lady never talked to us, really," Malik snorted, "let alone remembered our birthday."

"Yeah, it wasn't like she had to remember more than one," Jamal added, "since we were born on the same day."

A sad expression passed over their mother's face. "Like

I said, she went through some things. And she was never the same after. I'm sorry you didn't meet her when she was younger. She wasn't always so withdrawn."

"Yeah, me too," Malik said, casting his gaze down. "Mom, sorry I said that. It wasn't very nice."

She shook her head. "No, you deserved better." She patted his box. "But maybe this will make up for it."

Then she slid an official-looking document across the table.

From the Estate of Norah J. Wilkins.

Jamal's eyes scanned the document with the fancy lawyer logo at the top.

"This is from the attorney representing her estate," their mother continued. "You each have to sign to confirm receipt of your inheritance."

Jamal quickly scrawled his name. The pen felt slippery in his sweaty fingers. Then he passed it to his brother. His attention returned to the mystery boxes. Anticipation built inside him like water rising behind a levee, threatening to break through it.

"Okay, Malik first," their mother said, as if this wasn't always how it went. "Go ahead, Son. Open it."

Malik took a deep breath, then slowly cracked open the wooden box. The top pivoted smoothly on hinges built into the box, revealing—

A trumpet.

An antique one, from the looks of it. The brassy surface shimmered like it had just been polished to a high shine.

"Oh, cool!" Malik said, lifting it out of the velvet-lined interior. He raised it to his lips and blew a few tentative notes. They sailed out effortlessly, painting the air with their melody.

"Wow, it sounds amazing," Malik said. He played a few more notes.

"That trumpet has been in our family for generations," their mother explained. "Your grandfather was a jazz musician. And his father. And his father's father. They were all jazz musicians who played the trumpet."

"And then your mother married me," their father said with a chuckle. He held up his large hands. "Ever heard of two left feet? I've got two left hands."

"Yeah, but you can cook like a fiend," their mother said with a twinkle in her dark eyes. "I'll take that any day."

They locked eyes and smiled, lovey-dovey as always.

"Uh, is it my turn now?" Jamal asked, feeling like he might burst if he had to wait even a second longer.

His mom looked over in surprise, almost like she had forgotten he was still sitting there. "Oh, right, Jamal. Your turn. Go ahead, open your gift."

Jamal licked his lips, feeling a rush of adrenaline. He tasted metal on his tongue. He glanced over at the trumpet, feeling even more excited. If Malik got something that cool, then he was willing to bet whatever was in his box was good.

Slowly, he cracked open the lid. A musty odor drifted out, making his nose itch. He sneezed sharply. His watering eyes fell on the gift inside. It was . . .

A necklace.

And not just any necklace—he realized as he lifted it out of the box—a creepy old skull necklace. He ran his fingers over the skull. Its smooth texture sent an awful shiver up his arm.

Was it carved from real bone?

The skull hung from a thick chain with feathers and beads affixed to it, giving the whole piece an even creepier appearance. Jamal felt repulsed by the gift. He couldn't help it. He didn't even wear jewelry, let alone something like this. It was beyond ugly. Also, if he wore it to school, he was sure to get Colton's attention—and not in a good way.

That's the last thing I need.

He glanced at Malik, who was still focused on his trumpet. Envy stirred in Jamal's heart for the millionth time. It just wasn't fair.

Why did his brother get the *perfect* gift, while his grandmother left him a stupid necklace? He couldn't win.

"Well, would you look at that," his mom said, gazing at the necklace. Her eyes teared up. "Your grandmother left you her *special* necklace. You know, she never took that off. She wore it until she died."

"Uh, yeah," Jamal forced himself to say. "That's so . . . *thoughtful* of her."

He wanted to say something else. Something less nice. But he knew better than to upset his mother and held it in.

"Look, there's a note," Malik said, pointing at Jamal's box.

Sure enough, a card was nestled inside the red velvet

lining. Jamal lifted it out. It was printed on thick cardstock embossed with his grandmother's initials. Her ornate cursive handwriting stained the cream-colored card.

Beware of the shadows.
This will protect you.

Jamal frowned at her note. What did it mean? It didn't make any sense. But then he remembered what his mother had said about his grandmother not being right in the head, especially near the end of her life. The skull necklace, the card . . . they probably didn't mean anything.

"Weird old woman," he muttered, careful not to let his mother hear him.

Malik started playing his trumpet, whipping out an old jazz standard. With the new instrument, his brother sounded even better than ever. His parents clapped enthusiastically, transfixed by his brother's playing. "Play another song!" they exclaimed.

Jamal wanted to clap, too, but he couldn't bring himself to do it. Envy was a powerful brew, bitter but strangely tasty. Why did Malik always have to be so good at everything and get all the attention? Any plan to show his story to his parents evaporated. They'd never even read it.

Jamal was about to throw the skull necklace back into the box, annoyed that he'd been tricked into thinking something good might actually happen to him for once, when suddenly the skull's eye sockets flickered with red light.

Jamal jerked his hand back in shock. Had he really just seen that?

He glanced at his parents to see if they had witnessed the flash of light, but they were too busy watching his brother play his new trumpet. They weren't even paying attention to Jamal.

His heart thumped in his chest as he stared at the skull. Had it really just . . . *glowed*? Or were his eyes playing tricks on him?

He had to find out.

4

THE SHADOW MAN

Clutching the skull necklace to his chest, Jamal snatched the wooden box and note from the table and bolted for his room. Fortunately, his brother was playing another old jazz tune on his new trumpet. That meant his parents would be distracted and Jamal could be alone.

Jamal shut the door behind him. His heart thumped fast in his chest, reminding him of how he had felt when he saw those dolls watching him from the shop window. He flopped down onto his bed to examine the necklace closer. He ran his fingers over the skull, feeling the indentations of the eye sockets.

"Come on, do it again," he whispered to the necklace,

looking for a button or switch or battery chamber that could explain the flicker of light. But the skull's eye sockets remained dark.

No flash of light.

Nothing.

It was just a weird necklace. He studied the note again. *Beware of the shadows. This will protect you.* He read it over and over until the words blurred together, but still no meaning revealed itself to him. He checked the box, too. Maybe there was a secret panel? Or some other clue about the necklace and why it glowed with red light?

But still *nothing*.

Disappointment coursed through him for the thousandth time that day. Maybe his eyes were playing tricks on him after all. Just like with the dolls. He sighed.

"Stupid hunk of junk," he muttered, feeling angry. He shoved himself off the bed and stood over the trash can. He just wanted to be rid of it. "What do I need with a gross, ugly skull necklace anyway?"

He hit the trash can's pedal with his foot and the top gaped open. But the second he thrust the necklace over the can, the eye sockets began to glow again.

Jamal froze, afraid to move in case it made the light die out. He stared at the skull, making sure what he saw was real. The eye sockets glowed with eerie red light, like something demonic.

"How in the . . ." Jamal removed his foot from the trash can pedal. The lid slammed shut.

Only then did the necklace stop glowing. The light slowly faded until the eye sockets were dark again. But this time, there was no mistaking what he had seen. The necklace had definitely been glowing with mysterious light. He couldn't explain it, but it was real.

On impulse, he fastened the chain around his neck, feeling the weight of the skull dangling from it. He remembered his mother saying that his grandmother had *never* taken it off.

"Protection, huh?" he said, his eyes flicking back to the strange note.

Even though he didn't understand it, he could use some protection, right? He thought of Colton bullying him. Maybe the necklace could help. Not like he had anything left to lose. He tucked it under his shirt to hide it. He didn't want anyone to see him wearing it. After all, it looked weird.

Still he felt uneasy, remembering the skull's glowing red eye sockets. If it could do that, then what else could it do?

* * *

"Hey, wait for me!" Jamal yelled as the school bus's door began to close. But the door slammed right in his face and the bus left without him, speeding off in a noxious cloud of exhaust. He ran after it, but he wasn't fast enough to catch up. The driver didn't even notice him.

What else was new?

The last thing he saw was Riley watching him through the back window as the bus careened around a corner, leaving him alone on the curb in front of the school. His heart sank.

"Invisibility powers strike again," Jamal muttered, staring at his own shadow stretching across the asphalt. He wished more than anything that he could be sitting on that bus next to Riley, bantering away about their school day.

The bus vanished from his view, swallowed up by the busy city streets. The sun beat down on his back without mercy, clinging to the pinnacle of the sky. That hurricane was still building in the Gulf, but no one would know it from the clear blue overhead.

Even though it was one of those classic sweltering New Orleans days, Jamal would have to walk home. His mom had to pull a long shift at the hospital where she worked as an administrator, and his father was at the car dealership where he worked as a salesman. Barring a real emergency, they wouldn't be able to pick him up. Missing the school bus certainly didn't count as an emergency in their books.

He could already hear his father's stern voice: *Son, maybe if you walk home, you'll learn not to be late for the bus.*

But it wasn't his fault. For some reason, the bus driver never seemed to notice him, even when he was there on time. This was just the final insult in another terrible day at school.

"Lot of good you did today," he said, feeling the skull necklace under his shirt, his fingers slipping over the eye sockets. He'd worn the ugly thing to school, keeping it hidden under his shirt, in hopes that it would help.

According to his grandmother's note, it was supposed to protect him.

But protect him from what?

Certainly not getting left on the curb by the school bus and having to trudge home in the oppressive heat. Even worse, Colton had been giving him the evil eye all through gym class. Clearly, he was still furious about the previous day. Only Malik's presence had prevented Colton and his crew from doing something about it. But his brother wouldn't always be around.

Sooner or later, Colton would get Jamal alone. And then all bets would be off.

Jamal felt his stomach churn at that thought. He tried to push it from his mind and cheer himself up. Maybe walking home would clear his head and rid him of those worries for a while. Also, if there was one good thing in his life, it was the city where he lived. Despite the humidity and threat from hurricanes, he loved New Orleans—the parades, the food, the music, even the tourists who crowded the cobblestone streets in the French Quarter, who were always good for the people-watching that helped him create characters for his writing. There was no other place like it in the world.

He passed through Washington Square. As he walked by Tiana's, the most delectable smells drifted from inside. Jamal's mouth watered as he cut through the crowds, weaving down the busy streets. But even the vendors selling beignets and steaming cups of gumbo and musicians playing jazz music couldn't brighten his mood.

With each step, more sweat dripped down his back and the skull necklace thumped against his chest. Demoralized and overheated, he rounded the next corner and cut through a back alley—where he bumped right into the bullies from school.

"Look, it's Invisible Boy!" Colton sneered when he saw Jamal.

They were eating beignets, their lips dusted with powdered sugar.

"Where's your big brother now?" Colton said, tossing his blond bangs out of his face and advancing on Jamal.

The bully clenched his fists.

Jamal tried to back away, but the other kids flanked Colton, blocking any escape route. He was trapped. He glanced around, but the alley was deserted. There was nobody nearby to help. Not that anyone would have noticed him anyway.

"He's not here to protect you now," Colton said. "Whatcha gonna do?"

"Look, I really don't want any t-trouble—" Jamal stammered, scared. His back hit the brick wall. There was nowhere to run.

"You should've thought of that yesterday," Colton growled, "and taken your punishment for making us lose."

The other kids circled around, trapping Jamal. Adrenaline rushed through his veins, making his heart pound. Desperately, he reached into his shirt and pulled out the skull necklace. He thrust it up in front of Colton.

"Okay, do your thing!" Jamal muttered to the necklace. "Protect me!"

The skull dangled from his hands, swaying slightly. But *nothing* happened. The necklace didn't glow. The bullies burst out laughing. Colton most of all.

"Look, he's wearing a necklace," he said, doubling over with laughter.

But the necklace did one thing that helped—it distracted the bullies. While they were busy catching their breath, Jamal ducked around Colton and bolted down the alley. He ran as fast as he could, but he heard their pounding feet behind him.

Fortunately, he knew those streets like the back of his hand. He darted into the next alley, tore around the corner past street vendors and befuddled tourists, and ran into another alley. This one was darker and completely deserted. It snaked past the shop he'd seen from the bus the other day. The one with the creepy dolls in the window.

But he didn't have time to worry about that. There was a large dumpster in the alleyway. It smelled like . . . *bad* things. *Rotten* things. *Putrid* things.

Jamal ducked behind it anyway and held his breath, pinching his nostrils shut. Sweat slicked his skin and dripped down his face, stinging his eyes. His feet sloshed into an oily, stinking puddle. He felt the water seeping into his sneakers.

Please, run past me, he thought in desperation. If there was ever a good time to be invisible, this was it.

Sure enough, a few minutes later, the bullies bolted past the alley.

"Hey, where'd he go?" Colton yelled as they ran by. He sounded *furious*. "He's gonna pay for this!"

Jamal's stomach dropped. The next day at school would be even worse, but he would have to deal with that later. He held his breath and waited to make sure they were gone; then he crawled out from behind the dumpster.

Maybe Riley was right about invisibility powers being stronger, he thought. They did just save him—but at what cost? His shoes were soaked and stained black from that nasty puddle. His clothes were wet with sweat and smeared with grime from crouching behind the dumpster.

The necklace dangled uselessly from the chain around his neck. He ripped it off and held it up. The skull stared back at him.

"Protect me?" he sneered at it. "Yeah, right! Useless piece of junk. I'm not falling for that dumb trick again."

He was about to toss it into the dumpster when suddenly the eye sockets flared with light again. Much brighter than before.

"What the . . . ? Why *now*?" Jamal cried.

Suddenly, the shadows in the alley started to move and contort into monstrous shapes, like they were alive. Jamal froze in fear. Shadowy jaws snapped at him. The necklace flared brighter in response. The flare of light lit up the alley—and made the shadows vanish.

It was actually protecting him.

"What in the—" Jamal said, but then a dark silhouette suddenly stepped into the alley, blocking the entrance.

In the light cast by the necklace, the shadowy man slowly came into focus. He had dark skin, a thin black mustache, and a gap in the middle of his toothy smile. His arms and legs seemed impossibly long, giving him a skeletal appearance. He wore a black top hat with a skull and crossbones on it, as well as a purple feather sticking out of a sash tied above the brim. His purple coat with tails hugged his thin arms, his long black pants ended in a pair of shiny white shoes, and he held a cane with a purple crystal sphere on top.

Jamal stared at the strange man, terrified. His heart thudded, matching the pulsing light emanating from the necklace. The man's eyes fixed hungrily on the necklace. Quickly, Jamal fastened it around his neck again and tucked it under his shirt. He could feel heat emanating off it, singeing his skin and making him sweat more. It had never glowed so brightly before.

Jamal swallowed hard. "Who . . . who are you?"

5

ENCHANTÉ

"**G**reetings. *Enchanté*," the strange man said, tipping his hat toward Jamal. "A tip of the hat from Dr. Facilier."

He grinned, exposing all his teeth, but it looked predatory. Jamal stared at the necklace around the man's neck. It had two white fangs hanging from it. Everything about him sent chills down Jamal's spine.

"Little man, what's wrong?" Dr. Facilier said. "Cat got your tongue?"

Jamal knew it wasn't polite to ignore him. However, not talking to strangers—especially in scary back alleys— was the number one rule his parents had instilled in him. Also, the strange man gave him the *creeps*. There was really no other way to explain it. He felt like things were literally *creeping* all over his skin and making all the hairs stand up.

Not to mention the skull necklace around his neck continued to flare with light, even under his shirt, like a warning. It also felt hotter, like it was searing his skin.

Jamal started to back away. Suddenly, he wanted to be anywhere but standing in that deserted alley. The man's eyes narrowed, still fixed on him.

"Going so fast, little man?" Dr. Facilier said with a frown. "Don't be afraid. I just wanna talk. Were I a bettin' man—and I'm not; I stay away from games of chance—I'd wager I'm in the company of a very important person."

"Important? Who . . . me?" Jamal said in surprise. He had never been called important before. The necklace continued to flare with light, but he ignored it.

"That's VIP for short," the man added with a chuckle. He stuck out his hand. "You're Jamal, aren't you?"

"Wait, how do you know my name?" Jamal asked, wide-eyed.

"I know many things," Dr. Facilier said, resting his

hands on his crystal-topped cane. "Including that you have something that belongs to me. A necklace. And I want it back."

Jamal stammered. "N-n-necklace? What necklace?"

"Don't waste my time, little man," he said coolly. He held out his hand. His long fingers looked skeletal. They reached toward Jamal's neck. "Your grandmother's necklace, please."

"Wait, how do you know it's my grandmother's?" Jamal said. He closed his fingers around the skull necklace under his shirt. It flared brighter and hotter.

"Didn't you hear me? I already told you, I know many things," Dr. Facilier said with a sigh.

"But she gave it to me," Jamal said.

"Right, and now I'd like you to give it to *me*. It's quite simple, really," the man said. "Besides, what does a kid like you want with a necklace like that?"

"It's not that I want it," Jamal said. "My mom would kill me if I gave it away. She said this was my grandmother's *special* necklace. She never took it off, until she died. . . ."

"A real pity," Dr. Facilier said, but something about his expression said he didn't really feel that way. "But she's passed on to the other side now. She won't care if you give it to me."

Jamal released his grip on the necklace. "I'm sorry, I can't help you."

"Fine, have it your way." Dr. Facilier shrugged. "I mean, she gives your twin brother a trumpet, but all you get is that necklace? How did *that* make you feel?" He smiled broadly, exposing all his teeth again. "You can tell me about it. Your grandmother gave your brother a better gift, didn't she?"

"But that's impossible," Jamal said in shock. "You can't possibly know that."

"I told you," the man said. "I know many, many things. It's not very fair, now is it?"

"Yeah, it stinks," Jamal said, unable to help himself. He tasted envy like bitter medicine on his tongue. "Malik always gets all the attention. And I get . . . well . . . it's almost like . . ."

Jamal knew he shouldn't be talking to this stranger, especially in a dark, isolated alley. But he couldn't help it. A compassionate look crossed the man's face.

"Like you're *invisible*?" Dr. Facilier said, arching his

eyebrow and leaning forward on his cane. "Or more like you're standing in your brother's shadow. Am I right?"

He leered at Jamal from under his top hat. Suddenly, his shadow seemed to stretch out over Jamal and envelop him in darkness. How was that possible? It was like it had a mind of its own.

Jamal felt a surge of self-pity. "Yeah, it's like Malik is standing in the light—and I'm stuck in his shadow."

"That's a terrible situation." Dr. Facilier nodded sympathetically. "Just awful. But maybe I can help you out of your bind. I'm a doctor, of sorts."

"What kind of doctor?" Jamal said, taking in his top hat, purple suit, and crystal-topped cane. "I've never seen a doctor that looks like . . . well . . . you."

Dr. Facilier grinned. "A *special* one. And I have a bargain for you, one you'll find hard to resist."

"A bargain?" Jamal said. "What kind of a bargain?"

"What if I could fix your little invisibility problem?" Dr. Facilier said, twirling his cane. "What if I could help you step out of the shadows and stand in the light for once?"

"Wait, you can do that?" Jamal said. "But how?"

"Let's just say I know things," the man said. "*Special* things. *Powerful* things. *Magical* things. That's why they call me the shadow man."

Jamal froze. His nana—his father's mother—used to tell him and Malik scary stories about someone called the shadow man when they were small. But he'd always thought that was all they were—stories. If this was really him, then this man had special powers. Hope overpowered his initial trepidation. *Maybe I don't have to stay in the shadows,* he thought. *Maybe Dr. Facilier can fix things.*

But then his necklace flared with red light, snapping him out of his trance. It burned his chest. He remembered his parents warning him not to talk to strangers.

"Look, thanks for the offer," Jamal said, backing away down the alley. "But I need to get home for dinner soon, or my parents will be worried about me."

"Don't disrespect me, little man," Dr. Facilier said, suddenly sounding far less polite. "Don't derogate or deride! My time is highly valuable. Besides, you clearly need my help."

"No, I don't," Jamal protested. "I'm fine, I swear—"

"And don't lie to me, either," Dr. Facilier said, snapping

his cane at Jamal. "What about those big ol' bullies chasing you down the alley? The ones who pick on you in gym class?"

"How do you know *everything* about me?" Jamal said, his stomach clenching at the memory. "And why do you care so much about what's wrong with my life?"

Dr. Facilier leaned forward and narrowed his eyes. "All your life you've been pushed around, haven't you?"

Jamal flinched. Dr. Facilier was right. Even worse, he had to face Colton at school the next day. That meant . . . bad things were in store for him.

Dr. Facilier reached into the pocket of his purple suit and produced a business card. He walked over and handed it to Jamal. It had a skull wearing a top hat on the front.

DOCTOR FACILIER
TAROT READINGS. CHARMS. POTIONS.
DREAMS MADE REAL.

As Jamal scanned the back of the card, his skull necklace flared brighter and hotter than ever, like it was warning him to run away. But still he lingered in the alley.

He felt torn. The card was tempting. Maybe this strange man could actually help him.

" 'Dreams made *real*'?" Jamal read, then looked up at the man. "What does that mean?"

Dr. Facilier grinned and pointed toward a narrow purple door in the dark alley. A chill ran through Jamal again. Had the door been there the whole time? He didn't remember seeing it before. It led into the shop with the creepy dolls. The one he had seen from the bus the day before. They had stared out from the front window. Their eyes had seemed to lock on to him, though that was impossible. They weren't alive.

They're just dolls.

Jamal shifted his gaze to the sign over the door. It was shaped like a top hat with a skull and crossbones, the same as Dr. Facilier's hat. It read:

DR. FACILIER'S VOODOO EMPORIUM

Three skulls sat under the sign. Dr. Facilier tipped his cane at the skulls.

Suddenly, they lit up with flames.

Jamal's eyes widened in fear. "H-how'd you do that?" he stammered.

"Step inside my shop, little man," Dr. Facilier said, "and I'll show you."

6

DR. FACILIER'S VOODOO EMPORIUM

"**F**ollow me, little man."

Dr. Facilier thrust open the heavy door to his shop, which creaked on its hinges, and ushered Jamal inside. Jamal ducked quickly under the three skulls that still burned with flames.

It's probably just a trick, Jamal thought. Like the street performers in the French Quarter who did magic tricks to dazzle tourists into giving them bills and loose change. His father had warned him about them.

"This way, my young friend," Dr. Facilier said, leading him deeper into the shop. It took a moment for Jamal's eyes to adjust to the darkness. Shadows cast by flickering candles curled and undulated. They almost looked *alive*.

His gaze passed over glass bottles of colorful potions, shrunken heads, dusty books piled on shelves, and the handmade dolls. The air smelled musty and stale, yet sweet and alluring at the same time.

The skull necklace around his neck throbbed with light. *Run, run, run,* it seemed to warn him. Everything about the shop felt strange and unnatural. It felt wrong. He *wanted* to run away as fast as his legs would carry him, but something stopped him. He clutched the business card tighter. *Dreams made real.* The promise echoed through his head. Dr. Facilier was right: he did need help.

He took a deep breath to steady his racing heart. "What is this place?"

"My humble business, of course," Dr. Facilier said, gesturing around with his cane. "This is where I do my *special* work."

Jamal's eyes darted to the dolls in the front window. Their faces were crude swatches of burlap fabric, and their eyes were mismatched buttons. Pins stuck out of their lumpy bodies. But that wasn't what caught his attention. Their faces were turned toward him. When he'd entered the shop, they had been facing away, staring out the front window.

How did that happen?

Jamal remembered how they had seemed to be watching him when he was on the school bus. Between that and the skull necklace burning his chest and flashing urgently with light, he started to feel like he'd made a mistake.

"Uh, I really should be going," he said, backing toward the door. The dolls' button eyes seemed to follow him, raising all the hairs on his arms. His heart thudded in his chest. "My parents will miss me if I don't get home for dinner. . . . They'll start to worry."

"But *will* your parents worry?" Dr. Facilier said with a sympathetic look. "They prefer your twin brother, don't they? You're invisible at home, too. You're always in his shadow."

"No, that's not true," Jamal said. "They love us both . . . equally."

"Are you sure about that?" Dr. Facilier said. Then he reached into his pocket and pulled out a fistful of purple dust, which he blew into the air. It swirled around them and then slowly resolved into images.

Jamal recognized them. They were scenes from his life. They materialized in the air around the shop and played out like scenes in a movie.

His parents cheering for his brother at a basketball game. His parents watching Malik play trumpet at a jazz recital. His parents at the dinner table praising Malik, but ignoring Jamal. The family photos of his brother crowding the mantel, but almost none of Jamal.

"Wait, how are you doing that?" Jamal said, backing farther away in fear. The images from his life kept playing anyway. A smile twisted Dr. Facilier's face.

"I told you I have special powers. My friends on the other side tell me secrets. Trust me, little man. I can help you."

Jamal wanted to run away. He wanted to listen to the skull necklace and its warning. But the images hypnotized him. It was true: his parents *did* prefer his twin brother.

"You can change this?" Jamal asked. "But how?"

Dr. Facilier gestured to a round table with a tablecloth, set on a pedestal and surrounded by red velvet-backed chairs. The whole setting was illuminated by a crystal chandelier. "Have a seat," he said, tipping his cane toward it. "I can read your future. I may even be able to change it for you. The shadow man can make your every dream come true."

"You can really do all that?" Jamal asked. He chewed his lower lip. He knew he should leave, but something tempted him. He thought about the bullies waiting for him at school the next day, the bus driver deserting him on the curb, the teachers who never called on him even though he knew the answers, and his empty yearbook pages. "You can help me?"

"Sit down and you'll find out," Dr. Facilier said, leading Jamal over to the table. They took a seat, and Facilier produced a deck of tarot cards. They looked old. He shuffled them with great skill, then fanned them out on the table.

"Take three cards," Dr. Facilier said. "Let's see what your future holds."

Jamal reached for the deck and carefully selected his first card, then a second and third, laying them facedown on the table in front of him.

With a flourish, Dr. Facilier flipped over the first card. It depicted two children, but one of them stood in front of the other. Dr. Facilier pointed to the card with his spindly finger.

"This card represents your past," he said. "Your brother was born *first*."

"He's my twin," Jamal said. "But you're right. He was born five minutes earlier than me. And he never lets me forget about it."

Dr. Facilier nodded and flipped over the second card. It showed one boy holding a trophy over his head while another boy stood in his shadow.

"This is your present situation," Dr. Facilier said. "You're always in your brother's shadow. That's why you feel invisible. That's why nobody ever notices you. He's the cause of your problems. But you could have this. . . ."

With that, he flipped over the third card. It showed the second boy holding a trophy, surrounded by adoring fans, while the first boy cowered in the shadows. The shadows weren't just normal shadows, either—they looked like shadowy monsters. Their dark fingers reached for the cowering boy.

"Is that what you want?" Dr. Facilier said, his eyes locking on Jamal.

"You can do that for me?" Jamal asked, mesmerized by the card.

Dr. Facilier blew more purple dust over Jamal. Suddenly, the scene from the third card came to life, offering Jamal everything he had ever wanted.

Jamal getting called on first when he raised his hand in science class. Jamal getting picked first for basketball teams in gym. The school bus door opening wide for him. His parents heaping praise on him for his stories at dinner. His pictures taking up the entire mantel.

"Little man, don't you want your dreams made real?" Dr. Facilier said. "Don't you want to step out from your brother's shadow and have this future?"

Jamal *did* want it. He watched the images swirl around him in the purple dust. But then they faded away.

"Wait, bring them back," Jamal said, feeling a stab of longing. "I do want it. . . . I really do!"

"Very good. All I require now is payment," Dr. Facilier said. "This kind of spell isn't free, you know. My friends on the other side don't work for nothing."

Jamal frowned. "But I don't have any money. I'm just a kid. I don't even get an allowance."

"Oh, we're not talking cash," Dr. Facilier said. "Though that can be useful. It has to be something of great importance and value to the dreamer."

"Great value?" Jamal said. "But I don't have anything valuable."

Dr. Facilier pointed to Jamal's shirt, where a flare of reddish light could be seen through the fabric. "That skull necklace would suffice. From your grandmother."

Jamal reached for it protectively. It felt hot and kept flashing. "Wait, but I still don't understand how you know about my grandmother. Or her necklace."

Dr. Facilier's smile twisted. "That necklace. For this future." He pointed to the third tarot card. "Don't waste my time, little man. How I know doesn't matter. Now hand it over."

He held out his hand, his thin fingers outstretched. Jamal swallowed hard. He knew it was wrong. His grandmother had left him the necklace for a reason, even if he didn't fully understand it. His mother would be angry with him if he gave it away to a stranger.

But his head felt foggy, like he'd just woken up from a

deep sleep. The images from the tarot cards continued to swirl through his head, almost like he was in a trance. He felt envy surge in his heart again. The shadow man was *right*. He was sick of being stuck in his brother's shadow. He wanted what the shadow man had shown him in the third tarot card. He wanted it more than he'd ever wanted anything in his whole life.

He took a deep breath, then pulled out the necklace and held it up. It looked even eerier than usual in the flickering candlelight. The skull's eye sockets still glowed with reddish light. The air in the shop felt heavy, almost smoky. Jamal reached for the clasp to unfasten it, and the dolls in the window snapped their heads around. Their button eyes were fixed hungrily on the skull necklace.

What am I doing here? Jamal thought in a panic. Suddenly, he could see clearly. His eyes darted around the shop.

"I'm sorry. . . . I can't do this," Jamal said, jumping up from his chair and running for the door. His heart thumped faster. "I really have to get home."

He yanked the door open and dashed into the dark

alley. The last thing he heard was Dr. Facilier's voice echoing after him.

He sounded *angry*.

"You'll regret this, little man!"

7

CLASS PRESIDENT

"**N**o, get off me!" Jamal screamed. But the creepy dolls chased him through the Voodoo Emporium. Their button eyes were fixed on the necklace around his neck. He bolted for the door, reaching out to grab the doorknob, but one of the dolls clung to his ankle, tripping him.

He went down hard.

Wham!

"You can't run from us!" the dolls shrieked. There were so many of them. "We'll get that necklace back!"

The dolls swarmed toward him, their button eyes glaring.

"No, stay away!" Jamal screamed.

FIENDS ON THE OTHER SIDE

One grabbed at his arm, another grabbed his leg, and another reached for his neck—and the skull necklace. The doll grasped the heavy chain, pulling it and strangling him.

"No, please . . . let me go," Jamal gasped. "I'll give you anything."

Suddenly, a dark, skeletal shadow with a top hat stretched over Jamal, who was writhing on the floor.

"That necklace belongs to me." Dr. Facilier's voice reverberated through the emporium. "You can't escape from my friends on the other side—"

Jamal woke with a start, struggling for breath. He blinked at the bright sunlight streaming through his window. He looked down. His sheets were damp with sweat and tangled around his arms and legs. The skull necklace was twisted around his neck, partially choking him.

That explained it.

"It was only a dream," he whispered to himself. His throat felt raw, like something really had choked him. "It wasn't real. Just a terrible nightmare."

But the details had been so *vivid*. The terrifying dolls chasing him through the shop and attacking him. The shadow stretching over him. Dr. Facilier's voice. Even stranger, the dream didn't fade like other dreams did when he awoke. It remained sharp in his mind.

He sat up in bed, untwisting the damp sheets from his body. He glanced over at his brother's bed to see if Malik had witnessed his night terror. But it was empty. He felt a rush of relief. That was a small miracle. The last thing he needed was to get teased by his brother on top of everything else.

Jamal could hear the shower running in the bathroom across the hall. Malik must have already gotten up for school.

He glanced at the clock on the bedside table. "Oh, no," he whispered. He was running late.

He jumped up and dove for the closet, where he caught sight of his reflection in the mirror on the door. His face looked *haunted*. Dark circles framed his eyes. His skin looked clammy. The skull necklace dangled from his neck on the heavy chain.

The eye sockets on the skull were dark—it wasn't glowing. In fact, it had stopped glowing the second he'd stepped outside of Dr. Facilier's shop. Jamal frowned at it.

"Why does he want you so badly?" he said to its reflection.

Suddenly, the bedroom door flew open. "Why does *who* want *what*?"

Jamal jerked around, his eyes falling on Malik, who was wrapped in a towel. His hair was still damp from the shower. He ran his hand through it, shaking off a spray of water.

"Uh, nothing," Jamal said, quickly pulling on a shirt and tucking the necklace underneath it so it was hidden from view. It was moments like that when he missed having his own room at their old house, before the hurricane flooded it.

"Okay, weirdo," Malik said with a roll of his eyes. He paraded to the closet. "But don't make me late for school. It's a big day, remember?"

Jamal frowned at his brother while he grabbed more clothes. "Big day?"

"What, are you living under a rock or something?" Malik said, shaking his head. He pulled on a T-shirt. "The election results?"

"Oh, right," Jamal said. The week before, their class

had voted for the next year's class officers. His brother had run for president, of course. Homemade posters featuring Malik's grinning face had been plastered along every school hallway for the past month.

Jamal didn't bother running, not even for something less important, like class secretary or treasurer. Nobody at school knew he existed, let alone would be willing to vote for him in an election.

"I'm sure you'll win," Jamal added, trying to force himself to sound happy for his brother. But it came out sounding sullen.

Oblivious, Malik cracked a cocky grin and pointed at his own reflection, like a politician. Both brothers stared into the mirror. Their reflections were side by side. They looked the same—they were identical twins, after all. Except Jamal looked glum, while Malik beamed.

"Yup," he agreed. "And then you'll have to call me Mr. President."

* * *

"The election results are in," Mrs. Perkins said, clutching them in her hand. She stared at the class through her huge glasses. "Please congratulate your new class president . . . Malik!"

Jamal sank down in his desk while all the other kids broke into thunderous applause. Malik stood up and launched into a victory speech, where he promised better snack machines in the cafeteria and more pizza pep rallies before basketball games.

Jamal knew he should be thrilled for his brother. Malik loved him and always supported him, even saving him from Colton and the gym class bullies. But all he felt was jealousy eating away at his heart. Combined with the guilt, it was even worse.

After announcing the other officers, Mrs. Perkins flicked off the lights and projected their lesson, casting the classroom into darkness. Jamal squinted in the dim light. Her shadow fell across the class . . . and then, suddenly, it moved.

The arms transformed into spindly, ghostly claws.

They reached for Jamal's neck . . . and the necklace.

"No, don't hurt me!" Jamal shrieked, leaping up and jumping back from the shadow. Under his shirt, the necklace flared with reddish light and singed his chest.

Everyone in class turned to stare at him.

"Look, he's scared of his own *shadow*!" Colton cracked.

The whole class broke into jeering laughter. A spitball smacked Jamal square in the forehead. It stuck, then slid wetly down his cheek.

Mrs. Perkins flicked on the lights, causing the shadow to vanish.

"Jamal . . . is everything okay?" she asked. Her forehead crinkled in concern.

"Uh, yeah . . . sorry," he muttered, sliding back behind his desk.

When the bell rang, Jamal darted into the hall, slipping by his brother. The fan club clamored around Malik, congratulating him on his victory. Jamal knew he should join them, but he couldn't bring himself to do it. Especially not after what had happened in class. Instead, he shrank into the shadows creeping down the hallway. But then it happened again: the shadows moved.

They transformed into spectral shapes, reaching for his neck.

Even his own shadow turned on him.

Sharp teeth.

Spindly arms.

Jagged claws.

The skull necklace under his shirt was glowing again. Jamal bolted down the hall, away from the monstrous shadows. But they chased after him, stretching down the hall with dark claws. They clung to the crevices and cracks in the corners, where the light didn't reach fully.

The shadow monsters were gaining on him.

Adrenaline coursing through him, Jamal cut around the corner. The skull necklace flared brighter. He thought about hiding in the janitor's closet or the bathroom, but that would make it worse. It was *darker* in there. Instead, he ran for the exit, bolting past the security guard, who yelled, "Hey, kid, get back here!"

But Jamal didn't care; he had to get away from the shadows.

He burst outside into the bright sunlight. Only then did the shadow monsters vanish. The second they hit the threshold of the door where sunlight fell, they evaporated like smoke.

The security guard chased after him, snagging his arm and yanking him back toward the school. "Wait, d-didn't you see them?" Jamal stammered. "I-I can't go back there."

The security guard frowned at him. His sweat-stained uniform stuck to his pudgy frame. "See what?" he growled, narrowing his eyes.

"The shadows . . . They were chasing me," Jamal managed. "I swear it."

"Nice try, kiddo," he said with a chuckle. "What I *saw* was you trying to skip school. You're lucky I'm just giving you a warning this time. Next time, it's straight to detention."

Jamal stared back into the school, his heart hammering in his chest. Sweat poured down his face. But there were no shadow monsters waiting to get him. The hallway looked completely normal. Stranger yet, the security guard hadn't been able to see them.

The guard gave him a funny look. "You okay? You look a little sick."

"Yeah . . . I'm fine," Jamal lied, blinking to clear his head. He knew he couldn't answer honestly. The guard wouldn't believe him. The truth was . . . he felt really far from fine.

Were his eyes playing tricks on him? Or was this the shadow man punishing him for running away?

* * *

"Next year's pep rallies are gonna be the bomb," Malik said, sitting at a packed table surrounded by his adoring fan club. "Just wait."

Still feeling shaken, Jamal tucked his head down and headed for the other side of the cafeteria with his lunch tray. "I wish that could be me for once," he whispered to himself.

At that moment, someone shoved him from behind.

Jamal tripped forward, his milk carton spilling all over him and soaking his clothes, but somehow he managed to stop himself before he hit the floor. Slowly, he turned.

"Look, Invisible Boy's talking to himself," Colton sneered, glaring at Jamal.

His friends cracked up.

"Just wait for gym class," Colton added in a low voice. He clenched his fists. "You're gonna pay big-time for your little escape act yesterday."

They left Jamal dripping with milk and dreading next period. He glanced over at Malik's table to see if there was an empty seat, but it was packed. There were even kids standing around the perimeter, just wanting to be close to his brother. Feeling dejected, Jamal slid into a seat at an empty table. He glanced around to make sure no one was watching him—not that he needed to worry.

After all, he was invisible.

Jamal pulled out the skull necklace to examine it. It hadn't warned him about Colton. The eye sockets remained dark. "Why aren't you glowing right now?" he whispered. "Why don't you protect me from Colton?"

The skull just stared back at him. He remembered how it had glowed around the shadow man, and then when the shadows attacked him in science class and the hallway.

His grandmother's message flashed through his head. *Beware of the shadows. This will protect you.*

That was when it clicked. The necklace wasn't supposed to protect him from everyday bullies; it was supposed to protect him from Dr. Facilier and whatever dark magic he had unleashed on Jamal. The shadow monsters had to be the shadow man's doing. He was probably mad that Jamal had refused to take his deal the day before.

That was also why the necklace hadn't glowed in the alley when Colton and his friends started to bully him. That was why it was dark now. It all made sense.

Also, that had to be why Dr. Facilier wanted it so badly. It held some kind of power over the shadow man, even though Jamal didn't understand it fully. But then another anxious thought raced into his head.

If the necklace really did have power over the shadow man, then what was Dr. Facilier willing to do to get it?

The shadow monsters might only be the beginning.

A hand grabbed his shoulder. Jamal jumped.

"Wow, you look like you've just seen a ghost," said someone with a familiar voice.

It was only Riley.

Her eyes fixed on the skull necklace, but he quickly tucked it away. "Mind if I join you?"

"It's a free country," Jamal said, hating how bitter he sounded. He wished he could be excited that Riley wanted to hang out with him, but he knew that once she met his brother she would forget about him. "Not like anyone else is clamoring for the privilege of sitting with me."

He couldn't help it. His eyes darted over to Malik and his fan club across the cafeteria. Riley followed his gaze to his twin brother.

"You know, there are worse things than eating alone," she said. "Trust me, this is my *fifth* school in the last two years. You get used to it, Invisible Boy."

"Ugh, you heard that?" Jamal actually wanted to disappear.

"Hey, I've been called worse," Riley said with a snort. "Plus, I told you, invisibility powers rule."

"If I'm so invisible, why can you see me?" Jamal asked, pushing his tray away. His appetite had fled, too.

"Because I know what it's like to feel invisible," Riley said, popping a chicken nugget in her mouth. "And at least you have a brother. I'm an only child, and it's not very cool. Especially when your dad has to move for work, which means you have to move, too."

"Yeah, that must be tough," Jamal said, feeling something strange. A hopeful stirring in his chest. He risked a glance at Riley. Their eyes met, and she smiled. A genuine smile that made her eyes crinkle at the corners. Was this what it was like to have a friend?

A real one?

"Well, I'm hoping this time we stay here," Riley went on. "My grandma lives out in the bayou. And my mama wants to be closer to her roots."

"Wow, in the bayou?" Jamal said. "I didn't realize anyone lived out there. I've just heard the old legends—the ones about the witches."

"Boo!" Riley said, making him jump. "And she's not a witch. Not in the way you're thinking. Not like the Salem stuff. Let's just say . . . Grandma is a bit different," she said with a mysterious smile. "But I love her. Sometimes I think she might be my best friend."

"That's pretty cool," Jamal said, wishing he'd had that kind of relationship with his grandmother. "Mine just died last month. We weren't very close. But she did leave me this. . . ."

He pulled the skull necklace out of his shirt. Riley's eyes fixed on it—and widened. It was almost like she recognized it, like she'd seen the necklace before. He opened his mouth to ask her about it when raucous cheering broke out across the cafeteria.

"My fellow classmates," Malik said, rising to his feet in an impromptu victory speech, "I want to thank you for the honor of being your class president next year."

Applause broke out, followed by cheers of "Go, Malik!" and "Mr. President!"

Riley rose to her feet and joined the class in clapping for Malik. She was no longer paying attention to Jamal. This was what always happened. Soon enough, she'd forget that he existed.

Jamal just couldn't stand it anymore, not after what he'd been through that day. "Sorry, but I've gotta go," he said to Riley before dumping his tray and fleeing from the cafeteria.

Riley watched him leave with a strange expression on her face. *So much for my chance at having an actual friend,* Jamal thought. Why did his brother always ruin everything for him?

He pulled up his hoodie and hurried into the hall, wishing he really could disappear. He was tempted to run away and skip school altogether. He could sneak out the back door and avoid the security guard this time. Gym class was his next period—and that meant he'd have to face Colton and his friends. It would be worse than the previous year's awful wedgie incident.

As he continued down the hall, it seemed to grow darker and more shadowy. His heart began to pound. How could he be so stupid and wander off alone? Suddenly, his shadow started to move on its own. It grabbed for Jamal's neck.

"Get off me!" he screamed, bolting down the hall. But unlike the earlier shadow monsters, he couldn't run from his *own* shadow.

It followed him, reaching for his neck again.

There was no way to escape it. He felt the shadow fingers close around his throat. They pressed down, harder . . . harder . . . strangling him. Stars danced in his vision. He felt like he was about to pass out when—

He reached for the skull necklace and pulled it out.

"Help . . . me . . . please," he choked out.

Suddenly, the necklace burst to life, igniting with red light.

The flare of light drowned out his shadow, making it vanish for a moment. The fingers disappeared from around his neck. He could breathe deeply. Swallowing oxygen like it was cool water, he dashed down the hall. He didn't want to wait to see if the shadow would come back and attack him again. Next time might be worse.

He felt certain it was the shadow man's doing. Dr. Facilier wanted that necklace, and he was willing to unleash those monsters on Jamal to get it.

8

THE DEATH CARD

"**So, I've got some big news,**" Malik announced once they were all seated around the dinner table and the steaming pot of jambalaya their father had made for dinner. Jamal's mouth watered at the aroma of sausage, rice, chicken, and spices.

The table was set with a tablecloth and candles that cast flickering light. Malik set his new trumpet on the table, where it gleamed like it had been freshly polished. It was his most prized possession. He carried it around the house with him, filling their cramped space with its bright notes and only putting it away in the case under his bed when he went to sleep.

"Is it good news?" Mom asked with a slight trill in her

voice. She clasped her hands together and gave him her undivided attention, her dark eyes dancing with excitement.

"Of course it's *good* news," Dad said with a chuckle, setting his newspaper aside. The front page warned of the hurricane in the Gulf. It was a category four storm and growing.

What his father didn't say was that when it came to Malik, it was *always* good news. He wouldn't have said the same thing if it was about his other son. Jamal sank lower in his seat, his stomach churning unhappily. He wasn't hungry anymore.

The shadow man was right, he thought with a frown. His parents did prefer his brother.

"I won the election!" Malik said, throwing his hands up.

Their parents clapped for him while he prattled on excitedly about his ambitious plans for the next school year. Even though he loved jambalaya, Jamal picked at the food on his plate.

"This calls for ice cream," Mom said, clearing their plates and parading over to the freezer. "Chocolate, your favorite!"

She brought them all bowls, but Jamal didn't want ice cream. That was how bad he felt. He pushed it around, watching it melt. He kept glancing at the corners of the room, which were dimly lit and full of shadows. Were they going to come to life and try to strangle him?

Every time one of them moved, he practically jumped out of his seat. Finally, he couldn't take it anymore. He bolted out of his chair and ran to the light switch, flicking it on.

Bright light flooded the dining room. Everyone stopped eating ice cream and turned to stare at him.

"Whatcha trying to do?" Dad said with a frown. "Burn everyone's eyes up?"

"B-but . . . the shadows . . ." Jamal stammered, realizing how crazy he sounded. "It was really dark—"

"Son, you don't need a spotlight to eat ice cream," Dad said. "Now turn that off and sit your butt down."

* * *

Jamal wanted to fall asleep, but the shadows in the dark bedroom kept him awake. He wished he could sleep with the light on, but when he had suggested it, Malik had just teased him. "Wait, are you afraid of the dark? Sheesh, don't be such a baby."

"Uh, I just like . . . a little light," Jamal said, feeling silly. His cheeks burned with shame. "You know, so I don't trip going to the bathroom."

"Man, no wonder Colton and his friends pick on you so much," Malik said, stashing his trumpet in the case, flipping the clasps shut, and sliding it under his bed. "Little J, you gotta grow up already. You know, I won't always be around to protect you."

That had settled it. Jamal kept the lights off. He didn't want to act like a baby in front of his brother, but Malik didn't understand what was happening to him. Jamal wished he could tell his brother the truth, but Malik wouldn't understand. Or worse yet, wouldn't believe him.

Jamal felt completely alone. Everything was always so easy for his brother. Why couldn't Malik understand that it was different for Jamal?

He tried to sleep, but he kept glancing at the shadows cast around the dark bedroom, certain they were going to attack. Frustrated, he reached for the necklace under his shirt.

"You'll protect me, right?" he whispered to the skull.

The dark eye sockets stared back at him but didn't offer an answer. Right when Jamal was about to drift off to sleep, he heard a strange noise coming from inside the closet.

Thump.

What was that? He bolted upright in bed, clutching for the necklace. The skull's eye sockets lit up with reddish light. They cast a steady glow over the room, driving back the shadows. They lit the way to the closet door. Jamal stared at it, straining to listen for the noise.

But it was silent.

He relaxed slightly. *I must be hearing things,* he thought.

But then it happened again.

Thump.

And that time the closet door rattled. Something was in there.

"Hey, did you hear that?" Jamal whispered to Malik, who was tucked in his bed, snoring away. "Wake up!"

But Malik just flipped over, mumbled something like "Shut up" in his sleep, and buried his head in the pillow.

Right, I don't need his help, Jamal reminded himself. He

needed to handle this on his own. His brother wouldn't always be around to protect him.

Holding the skull necklace in front of him like a protective talisman, he tiptoed toward the closet door. When he got closer, the door rattled again.

Thump.

Something was definitely in there. But what? His heart hammering, he reached for the doorknob and gripped it. He flung open the door.

But the closet was empty.

There was nothing in there.

Just piles of shoes and dirty clothes on the floor, pushed inside to hide them from their mother. He must be hearing things, he decided, breathing a sigh of relief. After all, he'd had a crazy day. He was about to shut the door when his eyes fell on something next to his sneakers, partially buried under a pile of dirty clothes.

"Wh-what is that?" Jamal whispered, scooping it up.

The light from the skull necklace fell over it.

It was a tarot card.

He held the card closer to the skull necklace, which illuminated it with reddish light. The card depicted a twisted, dark figure with long, slim legs and arms that tapered into claws.

A shadow monster.

Just like the ones he kept seeing everywhere. His eyes fixed on the word scrawled in ornate script.

Death

The skull necklace flared even brighter. This was Dr. Facilier's work. The card looked exactly like the ones he'd used to read Jamal's future.

But how had it gotten into his closet?

That was impossible. His heart pounding like it might jump out of his chest, Jamal dropped the card and slammed the closet door shut. He stood there, staring at it in shock.

Thump.

The closet door rattled.

"N-no, leave me alone!" Jamal cried, backing away. He tasted metal on his tongue, which only happened when he was really afraid.

Then the death card slid under the closet door. It landed right by his foot. The shadow monster's eyes stared at him. They lit up and started glowing with red-dish light.

Then the monster *moved*.

It cracked open its jaws, exposing rows of jagged sharp teeth like a shark's.

It snapped at Jamal's foot.

"No, get away," he said, kicking at the card.

But more tarot cards started shooting out from under the closet door, pelting him. He bolted from the bedroom and slammed the door, hoping he was safe. He breathed a sigh of relief.

It worked.

But then . . . *Thump.*

The bedroom door rattled, making him jump back. The cards started shooting out at him. He fled down the hallway, but as he ran past each door, more cards shot out from under them.

He had to get out of the house.

Jamal ran for the front door. He gripped the door-knob. Tarot cards pelted him, filling the living room with shadow monsters. His skull necklace flared brighter.

THE DEATH CARD

He twisted the doorknob and threw the door open, revealing a shadowy figure.

It blocked the doorway—and Jamal's only escape path.

The skeletal fingers extended toward him, reaching for his neck like spindly claws. Then a deep voice rang out. "Little man, you've got my necklace. And I want it back."

9

DREAMS MADE REAL

"**W**h-what are you doing out here?" Jamal stammered, backing away from Dr. Facilier. The skull on his necklace flared. "H-how do you know where I live?"

The shadow man grinned. His teeth glinted in the moonlight. He was standing on the front stoop, holding the cane with the crystal.

"*Enchanté*," Dr. Facilier said, tipping his top hat forward. He aimed his cane at Jamal's throat. "Haven't you figured it out yet? As long as you have my necklace, we're connected."

"My grandmother's necklace," Jamal said, reaching for it. His fingers clasped the skull. He could feel heat emanating from it. "The shadows. The tarot cards. You did that to me!"

He backed away in fear, but the shadow man only tilted his head back and chuckled. "Well, now, I can't take all the credit. I had a little help from my friends on the other side."

"Your *friends* did that?"

"They're *special* friends," Dr. Facilier said. "They help me get what I want. And right now I want that necklace from your grandmother."

"But I can't give it to you," Jamal protested. "My grandmother left it to me. I already told you. She wouldn't like it."

What he didn't say was that he was afraid of why the shadow man wanted the necklace so badly—and what he'd do with it. It clearly had special powers and could protect him.

"If you give me the necklace," Dr. Facilier said, "then all these terrible things will stop—and you'll no longer be in your brother's shadow."

With that, he produced the third tarot card again. It was the one that represented Jamal's potential future, where he stood in the spotlight and his brother was the one in the shadows. Jamal stared at the card, feeling how much he wanted it.

"That's what you want, isn't it?" Dr. Facilier said, seeing the expression on his face. "To be out of the shadows for a change? I can do that for you."

Jamal licked his lips. He was so tempted. But then the skull necklace flared again.

It was a warning.

But what if there was another way? To keep the necklace—and get the future depicted in the card?

"What if I could offer you another form of payment?" Jamal said, his voice wavering.

Dr. Facilier raised his eyebrows and tipped his hat. "A bargaining man, huh? What else could you possibly have that I'd want?"

"Right, wait here . . ." Jamal said. He dashed back into his house, trampling over the tarot cards littering the hallway floor. The shadow monsters stared up at him.

Guilt pooled in his gut, but he ignored it. *I have to do this,* he thought, running into his bedroom. He crept to his brother's bed, slipping and sliding on tarot cards.

Malik was still sound asleep with the pillow over his head. His muffled snores drifted out.

Jamal knelt down and reached under his brother's bed. His hands landed on the trumpet case. He slid it out, flipped the clasps, and cracked open the lid, revealing the trumpet.

"I'm really sorry," Jamal whispered, slipping the trumpet out of the case. "But I need this. . . . You don't understand what it's like. . . ."

He shut the case and slid it back under the bed. Then he ran outside, where he found Dr. Facilier waiting for him—not very patiently.

"Little man, this had better be worth it. My time is highly valuable."

Jamal held up the trumpet. Its brassy surface glinted in the pale moonlight. "Right, I can trade you this," he said, ignoring the terrible feeling in his gut.

Dr. Facilier frowned. "A trumpet? Now what would I want with that?"

"My grandmother left it to my brother," Jamal said. "We each got a gift from her estate. It must be valuable. It's old and has been in my family for many generations."

"Valuable, you say?" Dr. Facilier's lips twisted into a predatory grin.

"You said it had to be something of great importance and value to the dreamer." Jamal looked down in shame. "Well, this trumpet counts. It's my brother's most prized possession. And he's very important to me."

The shadow man's eyes shifted to Jamal's neck—where the skull necklace still glowed under his shirt. He seemed to be thinking it over.

Jamal's heart raced. Was the shadow man going to refuse the deal? But then a sly look passed over the man's angular face.

"Fine, you have yourself a deal," Dr. Facilier said with a tip of his top hat. "The trumpet, in exchange for this." He held up the tarot card with the promised future.

Jamal nodded and handed over the trumpet. When he did it, the skull necklace flared, but it was too late. Dr. Facilier grinned in the moonlight and raised his hand, clutching the trumpet. Then he produced more purple dust from his pocket and blew it into the air.

Wisps of purple smoke swirled, enveloping Jamal. The dolls materialized from the smoke, dancing around the shadow man. Were those his friends from the other side? They boogied in the moonlight to an exotic drumbeat and chanted strange incantations in a language Jamal had never heard before. Their button eyes locked on to him, sending a chill straight down his spine.

As the shadow man cast his spell, images whirled around them. Jamal winning at basketball. Reading his stories in front of an audience. Answering questions in science class. Riding the school bus home surrounded by adoring friends. The scenes were mesmerizing. He couldn't wait for it all to happen. Then the shadow man cackled.

"Enjoy your *dream made real*," he said, vanishing into a swirl of purple smoke with his troop of creepy dolls. Jamal was left alone, standing on the front stoop. His heart hammered. The sun was just beginning to peek over the horizon. It was morning.

He reached for the skull necklace. It was no longer glowing with reddish light now that the shadow man was gone. It felt cool. That was a relief. Maybe all his problems were solved after all. He hurried back into the house— and the hallway was clear.

No tarot cards. No shadow monsters. No sign of the shadow man's curse.

A smile crept over Jamal's face. He returned to his bedroom and slid into bed, elated. The images from his new future danced through his head to the beat of the shadow man and his friends. But they were immediately chased by guilt.

His eyes darted to the case under his brother's bed. He felt sick to his stomach. He couldn't believe that he had stolen his brother's trumpet. Malik was going to be so upset when he woke up and discovered that it was gone.

Worse yet, Jamal had made a deal with the shadow man. He felt acid burn his throat and swallowed hard. "I had to do it," he whispered to himself. "I didn't have a choice."

The guilt lingered, eating at him and making him toss and turn.

What had he just done?

But he couldn't help feeling excited about the future the shadow man had promised him. The images from Dr. Facilier's spell swirled through his head. Didn't his brother love him? Wouldn't Malik want him to be happy for once? His brother would have to understand, Jamal thought.

Though he tried to sleep, it was hard when he was this excited. It was almost like Christmas Eve. He couldn't wait to wake up and see how different things were.

Everything in his life was about to change.

Everything.

10

ONLY CHILD

Jamal was back in his grandmother's house. He could tell by the smell of it. Sweet and musty. The smell of decay. The shadows contorted as he wandered through the dark hallways. The ancient wooden floorboards creaked under his feet. He reached the end of the hall and pushed a door open.

Creak.

It swung heavily on its hinges. The room inside was lit only by pale moonlight shining through the cracks between the thick curtains covering the windows. A shadowy figure sat in a rocking chair. Her face was shrouded by black veils.

She hunched forward in her chair. The veils blew back

from her head, revealing her wrinkled, skeletal face. Her once warm, brown skin looked almost gray. She stared at him with milky eyes.

"Beware of the shadows," she moaned. "Don't mess with the shadow man—or you'll regret it."

Jamal backed away, terrified. "No, Grandma! I'm sorry!"

"Don't you know he's trouble, boy?" she moaned, rocking back and forth in her chair. "How dare you give my trumpet to that horrible man? You can't trust him!"

Jamal awoke with a start. He was in his bedroom. *It was only a bad dream.* Sunlight, bright and crisp, streamed through his window. No musty smell. No thick curtains. No moaning voice. He inhaled and exhaled, feeling his heart rate slow.

He glanced at the clock and jumped up. It was time to get ready for school. Jamal bounded to the closet and cracked open the door, and in a flash he remembered the tarot cards.

He felt a stab of fear, but as his eyes grazed the interior, he saw it was perfectly normal.

Nothing was amiss.

No tarot cards.

He remembered the shadow man standing on his front stoop. And he remembered stealing his brother's trumpet and making the deal with the man. But now that all seemed like a bad dream, too.

Whistling to himself, Jamal pulled on a jersey and some jeans. "Hey, Malik, you getting up for school?" he called to his brother's bed across the room.

But his brother didn't answer.

Jamal poked his head out of the closet. His eyes fell on his brother's bed. It was empty. No sign of Malik. Also, the bed was made, like nobody had slept in it the night before.

That's strange, Jamal thought. His brother never made his bed except when their mother threatened them during one of her manic cleaning binges after too much coffee.

His mind whirred through possibilities. Maybe Malik got up early for school, excited about his first day as their new class president. Perhaps that was also why he had made his bed. Just showing off for their parents for the millionth time, Jamal decided with a roll of his eyes.

"As if he's not already *perfect* enough," he snorted, traipsing into the kitchen, which smelled of coffee and burnt toast. That meant his mother instead of his father had attempted to make breakfast.

"Kiara, step away from the toaster," his father said, unplugging it and handling it with oven mitts. A puff of smoke emerged from the vents, filling the kitchen with a bitter aroma.

"Uh, smells extra toasty," Jamal said with a smirk.

"Sorry, baby," Mom said, looking chastised. "I was just trying to help."

Jamal sat down at the island. He eyed the burnt eggs in the skillet, then poured himself a bowl of cereal instead. It was never a good idea for his mom to cook. He couldn't bring himself to stomach it, but sometimes Malik would eat it, just to make her feel better.

"Where's Malik?" he asked, digging into his cereal.

His father busied himself scraping the burnt eggs from the skillet into the sink. He fired up the disposal, which almost drowned out his answer. "Uh, Malik who?"

"Is that one of your new friends?" Mom said, giving him a knowing look over her steaming cup of coffee. "I mean, you have so many. It's hard to keep track. Isn't that right?"

"Sure is," Dad said, chuckling. "You're the most popular kid at school."

"Me . . . popular?" Jamal snorted, and almost spit out his cereal. He was sure he'd heard them wrong over the disposal. "You're mixing me up with my brother."

"Brother?" Mom said with a laugh. "What brother?"

"Son, you're an only child," Dad added, sounding concerned.

Mom got her "something's up" look. She walked over and felt his forehead. "Jamal, are you feeling okay?"

He swiped her hand away. "Ha, very funny. Is it April Fools' Day?"

His parents both stared at him, looking worried. "Uh, you know . . . my brother," Jamal went on. "He was born five minutes before me. Never lets me forget it. He's my twin. *Malik*."

Now they looked even more worried. Jamal felt a strange sensation creep through his body. He sprang up and ran into the living room, to the bookshelf with all the family photos on it.

"Come look, over here . . ." he started, but the words dried up in his throat.

His eyes passed over the pictures. He couldn't believe what he saw.

Every single photo was of *him*. Jamal was now playing trumpet at the recital and shooting a layup to win the basketball game. He was holding a first-place trophy at the school science fair. The family portraits showed only the three of them—Mom, Dad, and Jamal. Even the baby pictures, which had always depicted two fat, cuddly baby boys, now showed only baby Jamal.

There were no pictures of Malik.

It was like his brother had been erased.

Like he had never existed at all.

Jamal darted into his bedroom. His parents followed him, looking really afraid now. Jamal started yanking the clothes out of Malik's dresser.

"Look, these are my brother's clothes," he said, pointing to them, then to the twin bed across the room. "And that's his bed over there. We share a bedroom."

"Son, those are *your* clothes," Dad said, shaking his

head. "And that bed is for when your friends sleep over. This is your room."

"Uh, my friends?" Jamal said. "But I don't have any friends really. I've never even had someone sleep over."

"What do you mean?" Dad said. "You've got a ton of friends. You just got voted class president."

"And we're so proud of you," Mom added. "You won in a landslide."

"No, Malik is the popular one," Jamal protested, backing away from them in fear. "My twin brother. He has all the friends. It's like he has a fan club or something."

He rifled through the items on the bookshelf and yanked out his yearbook. "Come look, over here . . ." He flipped to the superlatives. But instead of Malik's face everywhere, it was Jamal's.

"W-what happened to my brother?" he stammered, staring in shock at his picture and name over *Most Popular*. How was that possible?

"Jamal, you have to stop. You don't have a brother," Mom said. "I mean, I was there when you were born. I think I'd remember something like having another kid."

"Yeah, I was there, too," Dad added. "That's not exactly something you forget."

"And the day we had you was the happiest day of our lives," Mom added with a smile. "We're so proud of you, kiddo. We couldn't ask for a better kid."

"Maybe you should stay home from school today," Dad said. "I'm worried you might be running a fever. Maybe even hallucinating."

"No, I'm fine . . . really," Jamal said. "It was just a bad dream."

He pinched himself—*hard*. But this time, he didn't wake up. His parents were just as worried as before, and his brother was still gone. Jamal glanced down at the yearbook clutched in his hands. Instead of Malik, he saw himself on page after page, playing trumpet in the jazz band, smiling out of his basketball team picture, winning the top prize at the school science fair.

That was when he remembered the deal he'd made with the shadow man the night before. *That wasn't just a dream—it was real,* he realized with shock. He had stolen his brother's trumpet and given it to Dr. Facilier in exchange for the future he had been promised.

But this wasn't what I meant, he thought frantically.

He had wanted to step out of his brother's shadow and get a taste of what it was like to be popular. But he didn't mean for his brother to be erased entirely.

That wasn't the deal. He remembered Dr. Facilier's sly smile when he accepted the trumpet. Jamal reached for the skull necklace he wore. He remembered his grandmother's warning to stay away from the shadow man.

Jamal's stomach flipped. He felt sick, like he might vomit. One thought circled through his head.

What did I do last night?

11

TRADING PLACES

Jamal entered the school with terrible guilt clawing at his insides. *What did I do last night?* The question ran through his head on repeat, like a bad song you couldn't get out. Each time he thought it, his stomach twisted. He remembered his parents saying, "Who's Malik?"

They didn't even know his brother's name. That memory made him feel worse. He had to find a way to reverse the curse. This wasn't what he'd meant when he took Malik's trumpet and made the deal.

The skull necklace hung heavily around Jamal's neck. He reached for it and felt the outline of the skull. *I should have listened to you,* he thought glumly. *You tried to warn me.*

Suddenly, a jovial voice reverberated down the hall.

"Hey, look, it's Jamal," Colton called out when he saw him. He jogged down the hall to catch up to Jamal. He clapped him on the shoulders. "Hey, buddy, how's it going?"

Colton and the other bullies crowded around Jamal, who flinched in response. This had to be a trick.

"Uh, I'm sorry about the game," Jamal said. "I promise I'll do better next time and score more points."

Colton gave him a strange look, then snorted. "More points? Dude, you crushed the other team. You scored the most points ever. I swear, it must be like a school record."

"W-wait, I did?" Jamal stammered, looking around at the other kids.

"Yeah, and there was that sick layup to finish the game," Colton added, wrapping his arm around Jamal's shoulder and steering him down the hall through the crowd of students heading to class. He mimed swishing a shot. "Just an overachiever. You'll do better next time. Ha! Good one."

"Right, you know me," Jamal said, feeling like he was losing his mind. Colton and his friends *liked* him now?

And he had scored the most points in the basketball game?

It was like they were confusing him with *Malik*. Except in this world, there was no Malik. It was really like he had taken his brother's place. He was living in some alternate reality.

How is this possible?

As they strolled down the hall, more kids ran up to him.

"Jamal, sign my yearbook?"

"No, sign mine!"

"Hey! I was first."

A pen was thrust into his hand, and yearbooks cracked open in front of him for his signature. The kids looked at him expectantly. He scrawled his name again and again, and then something strange started to happen. His guilt dissolved, replaced by a new feeling—elation.

Was that how his brother felt all the time? Like a social media star? Being noticed and standing in the spotlight was so much better than lurking in the shadows. He looked up from signing, and his eyes fell on Riley. She was standing by her locker, loading books into her backpack. She gave him a disapproving look. Her dark brows twisted into a frown under her purple mohawk, and her nose crinkled up. His hand froze mid-signature. It was almost like she *knew* what he had done. But how was that possible?

Out of the corner of his eye, Jamal saw something that looked like his own shadow dart across the floor. He blinked hard, and when he looked back, it was gone. Instinctively, he reached for the skull necklace, but it was dark and cool.

He breathed a sigh of relief.

"Must be tough being most popular," Colton said, drawing his attention from the necklace. "Does your hand get tired signing all those autographs? Come on, or we'll be late for class."

Colton herded the fan club away and pulled Jamal toward science class. He turned back to the disappointed kids, still clutching their yearbooks. "Look, show's over, folks," Colton said. "He'll sign more at lunch."

* * *

"Mr. President, care to answer the question?" Mrs. Perkins said, calling on Jamal right away. He couldn't believe that his teacher had noticed his hand up for once. And she'd called him *Mr. President*. The other kids lowered their hands. "Does light behave as a particle or a wave?"

"Actually, according to Einstein's theory, it can behave like both," he replied.

While Jamal always paid attention in class and usually knew the answers, he almost never got a chance to display his knowledge. Most of the time, his brother got called on.

"Very good, but I shouldn't be surprised by my *best* student," Mrs. Perkins said with a chuckle. "By the way, congratulations on winning the election. I know you'll do a stellar job, just like you always do in my class."

"Uh . . . thanks, Mrs. P.," Jamal said, using his brother's nickname for their teacher—something he would never have done before. Only his brother had the charisma to pull that off. He half expected her to chastise him, but instead, she blushed and chuckled.

"Oh, you're such a joker."

Jamal couldn't believe it. A cockiness he had never known spread through him. It was like he could do anything and everyone loved it.

He turned back, hoping to catch Riley's attention. He

suddenly felt like he could make a good impression. But she just glowered at him, then buried herself in her composition notebook.

It was so weird. Before, he'd expected Riley to lose interest in him when she met his brother. That was what usually happened. People forgot he existed when Malik was around. *Literally.* But not Riley.

Everyone else seemed charmed by him and loved him, but she couldn't care less. In fact, it was almost like she disliked him now. The dark magic spell had worked on everyone else. Why was Riley different?

That was when he saw it again: the shadow slithering across the floor toward his desk. It passed Riley and headed straight for him. And then he heard a strange whisper.

"Help me . . . please."

Jamal jolted in his seat, feeling the familiar guilt, but then the buzzer went off, signaling the end of class. Mrs. Perkins flipped on the lights, and the shadow instantly vanished in the flood of brilliance that washed over the classroom.

Next up was English class, where Mr. Edwards

practically begged him to stand up and read his short story—the one that had an *A+* scrawled across it—to the entire class. Jamal read from his original composition, *The Prince and the Frog*. He reached the last line: "'And then they all lived happily ever after. The end.'"

Before his voice died out, the whole class stood up and gave him a standing ovation. "Future Pulitzer Prize winner right here," Mr. Edwards said, swiping away a tear.

"Wow. Thanks," Jamal said, clutching his story and taking a bow. His cheeks flushed with warmth, and pride flowed through him. It was almost enough to wash away the guilt.

At lunch, he ate with Colton at the popular table and signed more yearbooks until his hand ached; then in gym class he got picked first and scored the most points. They killed the other team. But Jamal kept noticing a strange shadow trailing him up and down the court.

He was having such a good time, it was easy to brush off the shadow as his own paranoia. Besides, the skull necklace was dark. It wasn't trying to warn him. He didn't have any reason to be afraid.

"Wow, you did score more points today," Colton said,

giving him an impressed look. "You weren't kidding. I didn't think that was possible, but you couldn't miss."

They headed for the locker room. He had no fears of another tighty-whities incident. No worries about getting bullied. This was hands down the single best day of his life. *Or it would have been,* he thought glumly, *if my brother could have been here.*

"Sorry, but it's my turn . . . just this once . . . then I'll fix it," Jamal whispered. "I promise. I'll find a way to make it right."

"Talking to someone?" Colton said, catching his eye.

Jamal flinched. "Uh, just my shadow," he said with a nervous laugh.

"Always a joker," Colton replied. "Come on, let's hit the showers."

When Jamal, wrapped in a towel, entered the locker room and headed for the showers, he noticed something strange. The shadow was following him—the one he'd noticed trailing him all day long. Jamal's heart raced. It had to be the shadow man's doing.

But what does Dr. Facilier want now?

He darted into the shower and closed the curtain, but

the shadow slipped underneath. It was shaped like a boy. The shadow reached its clawlike hands out toward Jamal.

"No, stay away," he hissed, backing up in fear.

Automatically, Jamal reached for the skull necklace around his neck. It had protected him from the shadow monsters before. But it wasn't glowing; the eye sockets were dark. That was strange. It always warned him when Dr. Facilier was nearby. Why wasn't it working?

The shadow monster cornered Jamal in the shower. The fingers stretched into sharp talons. It cracked its mouth open, as if to devour him. A strange, raspy voice emerged.

"Help me, Little J!"

It was Malik.

12

SHADOW BOY

"**P**lease . . . help me, Little J," rasped the shadow. The voice sounded creepy and distorted, but there was no mistaking it was Malik. His brother was the only one who used that nickname for him.

Jamal stared at the shadow in shock. "Malik . . . is that *you*?"

That explained why the skull necklace hadn't lit up. This wasn't the shadow man haunting him—it was his own *brother*.

Except his brother was now a walking, talking shadow.

"Wh-what happened to me?" Malik croaked, looking down at his shadow hands in dismay. "Nobody can see me—except for you. It's like I'm invisible. . . ."

"Well, now you know how it feels . . ." Jamal muttered despite his shock, though he immediately regretted it.

"Wait, what do you mean?" Malik rasped, taken aback.

"I'm sorry," Jamal said, feeling terrible. "It's just . . . that's how I've felt all this time. Like I'm invisible. Like I'm in your shadow. Only I didn't mean for it to happen like this. . . ."

"For what to happen—"

Suddenly, a hand slapped the shower curtain.

Jamal jumped back. Malik—shadow Malik—froze.

"Hey, Jamal, still in there?" Colton called through the curtain. "Who ya talking to? Your own *shadow*?" He chuckled, not realizing how close that was to the truth.

It took Jamal a moment to find his voice. "Uh, no one . . . just myself."

Colton laughed. "Listen, your fan club is waiting outside the locker room. There's a bunch of people who still need your autograph for their yearbooks."

"Oh, right," Jamal said. "Uh . . . tell them I'll be right out."

No one would believe him if he tried to explain that

the previous day he'd had a brother who then turned into a shadow. They'd just think he was crazy. He waited for Colton's footsteps to fade away as Colton headed out of the locker room. Then he turned back to his shadow brother.

"C'mon, Malik, we have to sneak out of here before they see us."

Quickly, Jamal yanked the shower curtain back. His heart hammered while he scanned the locker room for any signs of Colton or the other kids. "Follow me. . . ."

"Uh, not like I have a choice," Malik rasped. "I am a shadow. That's what we do. We follow people."

Despite his panic, Jamal felt a smirk creep over his lips. His brother always had that effect on him. He had the ability to make him laugh and lighten the situation, no matter how dire. Jamal remembered when their house flooded and they had to move out and share a bedroom. Malik was the one who had joked about it.

"Hey, at least we get to spend more time together now, right?" he said, surveying their much smaller room, stuffed with two twin beds.

"Ha, you actually want to spend more time with

me?" Jamal said, feeling self-conscious around his popular brother. He flopped down onto his bed. "What about your fan club?"

"Very funny," Malik said with a laugh, but then he turned more serious. Their eyes met. "And of course I do. You're my *only* brother—and *best* friend. And that's forever, Little J."

Remembering that made Jamal feel even worse. *I'll find a way to make this right,* he thought with regret. *I promise.*

As quietly as possible, Jamal crept through the locker room. Malik slipped under the shower curtain and flowed over the concrete floor after him. The locker room was deserted, fortunately. Jamal quickly slipped back into his street clothes, then headed for the back exit that led outside. The locker room was dark and shadowy. Jamal kept his eyes on the shadows, watching for any unusual movement or sign that Dr. Facilier was around. But nothing moved—except him and his shadow brother.

Suddenly, he heard Colton's voice again. Jamal froze and ducked behind the nearest row of lockers, crouching down to hide.

"Yo, Jamal . . . you coming?" Colton yelled.

"Just one more minute," Jamal called out.

"Okay," Colton said. "But you're gonna be late for next period if you don't hurry up."

Jamal waited for his footsteps to fade, then turned to Malik. "Come on. This way," he hissed to his shadow brother, pushing open the exit door. "Before anyone sees us."

Bright sunlight flooded through the doorframe, falling over the deserted locker room. Jamal blinked hard, then hurried out onto the athletic field. His brother flowed over the freshly mowed grass and stuck close to him like . . . well . . . like a shadow. Overhead, the sun beat down on them, making Malik's shadow darker and more defined.

Jamal ducked behind the field house, where they stored the sports equipment. Malik followed, and reached his shadowy hands out toward Jamal as if for help, but they passed through him. Malik couldn't touch his brother.

"Little J, you have to help me," Malik rasped, throwing his hands down in frustration. "I don't know what happened to me. This morning, I woke up like this. I've been following you around all day, trying to get your attention. Nobody can see or hear me—except for you."

Jamal felt another stab. He'd been so wrapped up in being popular and having everyone clamor for his autograph that he hadn't noticed his poor brother trying to get his attention. That explained the strange shadow he kept seeing and whispers he'd been hearing all day.

It was my poor cursed brother—cursed because of me.

"Malik, I-I'm so sorry," Jamal stammered. "It's all my fault."

"Your fault?" Malik rasped in surprise. "But how's that possible?"

"Well, it's a long story," Jamal confessed. "But I guess I've always been jealous of you. . . ." He trailed off, the words drying up in his throat and turning into dust.

"Jealous . . . of me?" Malik said, taken aback. "What do you mean?"

"Everything always comes so easily to you," Jamal said, pacing around. He ran his hands through his hair in frustration. "You're the most popular and best at everything. Just look at the yearbook. I guess I just wanted to know what that felt like for a change."

"Wait, you wanted to be like me?" Malik said in his creepy shadow voice. "But why would you want something like that? I know we're twins, but it's okay that we're different."

"Yeah, I guess I wanted to step out of your shadow," Jamal said. "When you're around, it's like nobody can see me. There isn't room for me to get noticed, even when I'm actually good at something, like science or writing stories. Or even basketball when you're not defending me."

"But Mrs. Perkins loves you," Malik croaked. "You get As in her class."

"Oh, yeah? Then why doesn't she ever call on me?" Jamal said, upset. "Even when I usually know the answer and raise my hand? She always calls on you first."

"She calls on you sometimes," Malik replied.

"Like when?" Jamal demanded. "You see? I may as well be invisible."

The tension between them sizzled in the air like electricity. They had never argued like this before, and they both knew it.

"Okay, maybe you have a point," Malik rasped finally.

"She does usually call on me first. But who cares about boring science stuff, anyway?"

Jamal thumped his chest. "Me . . . I care! I love science. It's my favorite subject. And what about basketball? I always get picked last, while you get picked first every time."

"Fine, but that doesn't mean you had to do this to me," Malik said, sounding hurt and angry. His shadow form twisted on the ground. "Spit it out already. What happened?"

Jamal started pacing again. His feet trampled the manicured grass. "Listen, all I wanted was to feel what it was like to get noticed for once. But I didn't mean for him to turn you into an actual shadow. He tricked me. This isn't what I meant to happen."

"Who are you talking about?" Malik said.

His shadow form lightened and vanished for a second as a cloud passed over the sun. "Malik, come back!" Jamal said, afraid that his brother had vanished for good.

But as soon as the sun returned, Malik reappeared as well. His voice was also restored as soon as he rematerialized, like the volume being turned up on a speaker.

"Who are you talking about?" Malik demanded. "Who did this to me?"

Jamal swallowed hard. "Dr. Facilier . . . he's the shadow man."

"Wait, you made a deal with the *shadow man*?" Malik said in a horrified voice. "What were you thinking? You can't mess with that kind of dark magic. You know that!"

"You have to understand—he tricked me," Jamal said. "This wasn't our deal."

"But you can't trust the shadow man! Nana warned us about him," Malik rasped angrily. "No wonder this happened. How could you be so stupid? I can't believe *my own brother* did this to me."

Malik's words stabbed him like a knife to the heart.

"I'm . . . I'm so sorry," Jamal stammered. "I never should've talked to him. I didn't mean for this to happen. I think Grandma tried to warn me, too, but I didn't understand her message."

" 'Beware of the shadows,' " Malik said, recalling the words from the note their mom's mother had left behind with the necklace. The anger faded slightly from his voice and was replaced by curiosity. "You think Grandma was warning you about Dr. Facilier?"

Jamal nodded. "Yeah, I think so, only I didn't understand." He pulled out the skull necklace to show it to Malik. "This necklace she gave me glows whenever he's around and protects me from his shadows. It's the reason Dr. Facilier came after me in the first place. He wants this necklace—and he seems willing to do anything to get it."

"But why does the shadow man want it so badly?" Malik rasped, cocking his head toward the skull necklace. "What's so important about it?"

"Right, that's the problem. I don't know," Jamal said. "Clearly it has some kind of power over him. Maybe he wants to get his hands on it so he can destroy it? I'll bet this was his plan all along, since I wouldn't give it to him. I'm so stupid. I knew I couldn't trust him."

"So he turned me into a shadow to trick you?" Malik responded.

"Yeah, he told me that I would get to step out of your shadow if I gave him something valuable," Jamal said, remembering their deal. "So I snuck under your bed while you were asleep, and stole your trumpet and gave it to him. The one Grandma left to you—"

Malik cut him off, sounding furious. "Wait, not only did you make a deal with the shadow man, but you stole my trumpet to do it? Little J, how could you?" His shadow form twisted.

Jamal swallowed hard. "I knew it was wrong, but you have to understand . . . all I wanted was to know what it would be like to walk in your shoes for one day. But he didn't tell me that he'd turn you into an *actual* shadow. I never would've made the deal if I'd known the truth."

"Dark magic always backfires," Malik said, shaking his shadow head. His voice still wavered with fury. "This is, like, basic stuff."

"Yeah, it's official," Jamal said, looking down at his shadow brother. "I'm the worst brother ever. I really messed this up. But I swear—I'll find a way to fix it. Maybe if I give him the skull necklace, then Dr. Facilier will agree to reverse the curse and bring you back."

Malik hesitated. His shadow form lightened and faded again as another cloud passed over the sun. Jamal's heart squeezed with fear, but then Malik reappeared.

"Jamal, reversing the curse doesn't change what you did to me," Malik said, looking down at his shadow hands. "Honestly, I don't know if I can ever trust you again."

Jamal couldn't believe it. His brother had used his real name. *Jamal.* Not his nickname. Malik almost never called him by his real name. That meant he was seriously upset.

Jamal felt beyond terrible—and worse yet, he knew that Malik was right. *How could I have done this to my own brother?* he thought, feeling sick to his stomach. If he didn't find a way to fix it, then his parents might never remember having another son. He and Malik might never share a bedroom again or play pranks and mess around with each other.

But more than that, Jamal would lose his best friend.

"Please, I'll make it right," Jamal begged, fighting back tears. "Just give me a chance. We can reverse the curse. Then Mom and Dad and everyone will have to remember you."

"I don't know," Malik rasped. "Also, we have to find out why the shadow man wants that necklace. Grandma left it to you for a reason. What makes it so valuable? What power does it have?"

Jamal frowned. "Yeah, you're right. It could be dangerous."

"I mean, clearly the shadow man can't be trusted," Malik warned, thinking it over. "It could be really bad if we give it to him, right? Or what if he double-crosses you again?"

Suddenly, a shadow fell over them. A real one this time.

Then a voice rang out, making them both jump.

"Are you talking about that creepy old skull necklace?"

13

THE BAYOU

At first, Jamal was certain Dr. Facilier was about to pounce.

But his eyes fell on . . . *Riley.*

She was standing behind them. She cocked her head. Her eyes were locked on the skull necklace. In the bright sunlight, her hair looked even more vibrantly purple than usual and her brown skin almost glowed.

"You know, that isn't just any ordinary necklace," she said. "So be careful with it. It's dangerous to just pull it out in broad daylight like that. Somebody might try to steal it."

"W-wait, what?" Jamal stammered, clutching the

necklace tighter in his fist. "How do you know about my necklace? And, well . . . yeah . . . that already happened."

Riley frowned. Her eyes darted to the shadow at Jamal's feet.

"Also, why're you talking to your own shadow?" she asked.

"Uh, you heard that, too?" Jamal said, feeling self-conscious. Blood rushed to his cheeks, making them hot.

"Yeah, not much escapes my notice," Riley added with a smirk. "I've been watching you. And today you were acting super weirdo. Like next-level weirder than usual. Then I noticed when you didn't come out of the locker room after gym class."

"So you followed me out here?" Jamal said.

"Yeah, don't worry. I'm not a stalker," Riley said with a dramatic eye roll. "Just curious. Plus, I pay attention when my friends are acting like something's wrong."

Friends. She actually thought of him as a friend.

"But why are you so interested in me?" Jamal asked. "Why are you the only one who seems to notice me?"

Riley shrugged. "I dunno, to be honest. But my whole life, I've been *different*. It kind of runs in my family, I guess. I can see things that nobody else can. So can my grandmother."

Jamal took that in. He felt like she was a kindred spirit. He had always felt different, too. Though he'd never had any superpowers . . . until the skull necklace and the shadow man.

"Also, I noticed that skull necklace," Riley went on. "The other day in the cafeteria. The way you were pulling it out. I was worried you didn't know what it really was. . . ."

"The necklace?" Jamal said. "What do you know about it?"

"It has special powers," Riley said with a frown. "You gotta be careful with that stuff. You never know who might be drawn to it."

"Jamal, she knows about the necklace," Malik rasped excitedly, shifting around on the ground. "Maybe she knows something that can help us."

Riley flinched and her eyes widened in fear. She glanced from Jamal to the shadow at his feet. "What the . . . Your shadow . . . can talk?" she said in shock, her eyes fixing on Malik.

"Wait, you can hear me?" Malik rasped hopefully.

"Whoa! No way! You're Malik," she said, recognizing his voice. "Jamal's brother. But you're . . . a shadow?"

"You remember him?" Jamal asked.

"Of course I do," Riley said. "Why? What's going on?"

Jamal hesitated, unsure if he could trust Riley. He had only known her for a few days. But she was the only person in the entire school who remembered that Malik existed. That had to mean something. Plus she'd been nice to him from the day she'd arrived at school. There was definitely something different about her. And she seemed to know things about the necklace that he hadn't told anyone other than Malik. Maybe she had information that could help them.

And right now we need all the help we can get.

"Go ahead, spit it out," Riley said with an impatient sigh. She crossed her arms and stared him down. "This day can't possibly get any weirder."

"Be careful what you wish for," Malik rasped. Even as a shadow, he still had his dry sense of humor.

"Literally," Jamal said with a frown. "Okay, it's a long story. . . ."

Jamal glanced around to make sure that nobody was watching them, but the athletic field was deserted, because everyone was still in class. Bright sunlight beat down on them, but soon it would be late afternoon and the sun would start to fade. He glanced around, scanning for the security guard, but he wasn't lurking nearby.

So he took a deep breath and told Riley everything. He explained that Dr. Facilier had promised him that he could step out of his brother's shadow if he gave him the skull necklace. But the necklace always glowed to warn him about the shadow man. So he'd traded his brother's trumpet instead, but then he'd woken up and Malik was gone . . . until he revealed himself to be a shadow.

"We think he double-crossed me," Jamal finished, digging the toes of his shoes into the field. "This wasn't what I meant to happen when I made that deal."

"I can't believe you've been messing with the shadow man," Riley said, her voice wavering with fear. "You can't trust him. Everybody knows that."

"Okay, I get it," Jamal said, casting his gaze down. "I feel so stupid. I just wanted to know what it would feel like to have friends for once."

"But you did have a friend," Riley said in exasperation. "I'm your friend. Didn't you notice?"

Jamal's eyes darted to his brother. "Yeah, but you would've forgotten me, too, once you met my brother. That's what always happens. . . ."

Riley smirked. "Hey, hate to break it you. Your brother's cool and all that jazz, but I like you way better."

"Wait, you do?" Jamal said.

"Cross my heart and hope to die," Riley said.

"Uh, guys, I'm, like, right here," Malik rasped. "Even if I am a *shadow*, I can still hear you talking about me."

They all laughed—it felt good to laugh—but then Riley turned more serious. "Look, at least you didn't give Dr. Facilier that skull necklace. That would've been way worse."

"Uh, what could be worse than this?" Jamal said, pointing to his shadow brother. "Also, if he wants it so bad, why doesn't he just take it? Why go through all of this?"

Riley frowned and studied the necklace more closely. Her fingers stroked the eye sockets; then she looked up. "My best guess is that it's got a protection spell placed on it."

"Protection spell?" asked Malik.

Riley nodded. "You said it glows and warns you when the shadow man is nearby?"

"Yeah, that's right," Jamal confirmed. "Every single time."

"Well, then maybe it also has a spell placed on it to prevent him from taking it," Riley went on. "If that's the case, then the only way he can possess it is if you give it to him."

"That makes sense," Jamal said, thinking it over. "Only I'm going to have to give it to him now. It's the only leverage I've got to make him reverse the curse and bring Malik back. What other choice do I have?"

Riley chewed on her lower lip. "Look, I don't know everything about that necklace," she said, "but Grandma DeSeroux might know more. She has one just like it."

"Your grandmother has one, too?" Malik rasped. "That's crazy."

Riley nodded. "Yeah, and we need to go see her. She's . . . *special*. She lives deep in the bayou."

Jamal exchanged looks with Malik, then turned back to Riley.

"But the bayou is filled with gators and poisonous snakes," Jamal said.

But Riley had already started across the track toward the road.

"Just follow me. And bring your shadow brother with you." She gave them an annoyed look. "And don't be such scaredy-cats. I know the secret path through the bayou. My grandmother showed me the way."

"Uh, right, it's not like I have a choice whether to bring him," Jamal said, jogging to keep up with her. "He is a shadow now. He sort of follows me wherever I go. . . ."

They traversed the athletic field, slipped under the perimeter fence, and crossed the road, ducking to avoid being busted by the security guard for skipping school. As they headed for the thick trees that marked the edge of the bayou with shadow Malik trailing them, Jamal felt goose bumps prick the back of his neck. He got the feeling someone was watching them.

That was when the skull necklace lit up.

Jamal glanced back—and his eyes fell on Dr. Facilier. He was standing on the roof of the school, watching them. The creepy dolls surrounded him like a flock.

Their mismatched button eyes were also locked on them. They almost looked . . . *hungry*.

Dr. Facilier tipped his top hat toward Jamal. How much had he overheard?

Goose bumps erupted all over Jamal's body. He reached up and clutched the necklace. It felt warm. It probably did have some sort of protection placed on it so Dr. Facilier couldn't just take it from him. But it seemed like the shadow man was growing stronger.

Jamal couldn't explain exactly how he knew that. It was more of a feeling. Maybe because the necklace linked them together somehow.

But then they ducked into the bayou and were swallowed up by the trees. The shadow man vanished from Jamal's sight, but Jamal knew one thing for sure: Dr. Facilier was watching them.

He wants this necklace, Jamal thought with a shiver, *and I bet he's willing to do anything to get it back.*

14

GRANDMA DESEROUX

"**Y**ou know, people stay away from the bayou for a reason—" Jamal started, but then he tripped over a ropy cypress tree root arced out of the soggy earth. He lurched face-first toward a puddle, catching himself at the last minute.

His face was one inch from the putrid, murky water. Mud splashed onto his clothes and face. He tried not to imagine what disgusting creatures lurked underneath the surface.

"There's tons of Creole people and Cajun people who live out here," Riley called out. "They just know how to do it right and not gripe. Like some people."

She glanced back but didn't slow her pace. She was

agile and sure-footed as she led them through the marsh. And it was a good thing she knew the way. Jamal was already completely lost.

All around them spanned the massive wetlands. Brackish water that barely moved housed countless types of wildlife. Cypress and tupelo trees sprouted from the marshy ground. Though Jamal had grown up in New Orleans, he had never ventured this deep into the bayou. But Riley easily located the path that cut through the thick underbrush and led to her grandmother's hut.

"Easy for you to say," Jamal muttered, well, *griping* again. Even the path was hard to follow. "I've never been back here. And I'm starting to realize it was for a very good reason."

"Hey, remember what I said about *griping*?" Riley said.

"Uh, she's right," Malik rasped behind him. "Little J, you are being, like, a major punk right now."

"Even your shadow agrees," Riley said with a smirk. "Now hurry it up. It's gonna get dark soon. We don't have much time."

Jamal felt sweat erupt on his forehead. He remembered the shadow man, surrounded by his creepy dolls, watching them from the gym's roof. She was right: they had to act fast.

He cast his gaze ahead, feeling the muggy air slick his skin with sweat. Their surroundings were like an ancient jungle. Moss dripped off the cypress trees that stretched overhead toward the sky, while their exposed roots looped out of the wetlands.

The sun was beginning its nightly descent into the horizon. Already the sky was stained pink. Clouds were building. Night would fall soon, and with the coming darkness the odds of them getting lost were higher.

"Ouch, watch out," Jamal muttered as a branch smacked his cheek. It throbbed painfully.

"Griping again?" Riley said with a snort. "Toughen up, already."

"Well, there are a few good things about being a shadow," Malik observed, trailing Jamal. "No shoes. No splashing in puddles. And pretty sure poisonous snakes can't bite me."

"Uh, what kinds of snakes?" Jamal said, checking the marsh around his ankles.

"Cottonmouths. Copperheads. Rattlesnakes," Riley

said. "And don't forget about the gators. Though usually they mind their own business . . . if you mind yours."

"Just great," Jamal groaned. "What other horrors are lurking back here?"

"Relax, I've come this way a thousand times." She raised her arms over her head. "And look, I've still got all my limbs."

"I feel so much better," Jamal said, not comforted at all.

He marched forward anyway, following Riley. His brother, a dark smudge cast against the earth, trailed them. Malik vanished and reappeared with each patch of sunlight that filtered through the thick branches. Once the sun fell, it would be almost impossible to see him.

Every time his brother vanished, Jamal felt a thump of dread. He worried that this would be the time Malik vanished forever, and then he breathed a sigh of relief whenever Malik reappeared.

"Stay close," Jamal whispered to his brother. "I can't lose you . . . *again*."

"Close as your own shadow," Malik rasped back. "Don't worry, Little J."

Not only did his words reassure Jamal, but also his brother no longer seemed as angry with him. He was back to calling him Little J. Jamal felt a twinge of hope. Maybe if he did find a way to fix Malik, his brother would also find a way to forgive him.

He could hope, couldn't he? What other choice did he have?

"Riley, please tell me you know where you're going," Jamal said, trying to discern their path through the bayou. As it grew darker, it got harder to see. "And that we're not totally lost."

"Of course I do," Riley said with a derisive snort, not slowing her pace through the underbrush. "The bayou runs in my family's blood. Some of us never left, like my grandmother. Her hut is just up this way . . ." she said, tramping ahead through the standing water.

Jamal followed her, less certainly. Water sloshed up to his knees.

"You trust her?" Malik asked, startling Jamal. He still wasn't used to his brother being a shadow. He was nearly invisible in the darkness that was falling over the bayou.

"Uh, do we have a choice?" Jamal said, his gut churning with fear.

He was afraid, not just of the bayou and getting lost and whatever creepy, crawly, deadly creatures lurked underneath the brackish water, but also of what would happen if he didn't find a way to help his brother and reverse the shadow curse.

Fear for his brother overwhelmed his fear of the bayou, so he kept plodding forward despite his discomfort. Right now, Riley and her grandmother were their best—their *only*—hope.

As they continued, the sun descended, casting longer and deeper shadows across the swamp. Jamal could barely see the path. He strained his eyes in the fading light.

Suddenly, something moved in the darkness.

Jamal startled and whipped around. Something small and fast was moving through the underbrush. *Thwap. Thwap. Thwap.* And then the skull necklace started to glow. That could mean only one thing: the shadow man had found them.

"Riley, look!" Jamal yelled, holding up the skull.

The reddish light illuminated the shadows, lighting

up the bayou—and the button eyes staring back at them. Pair after pair of creepy eyes. There were too many of them to count.

"Oh, no, it's them," Riley yelped. She grabbed Jamal's hand and yanked him back, away from the staring eyes. "Hurry, run!"

"But who are they?" Jamal asked, struggling to keep up and not trip.

"The dolls," Riley repeated breathlessly, pulling him faster through the swamp. "They belong to the shadow man's friends on the other side. He must have asked his friends for their help and they summoned the dolls to do their bidding."

"Their bidding?" Jamal said.

"Yeah, they're probably after that necklace," Riley said. "We have to get to my grandmother's hut. She can protect us . . . or at least . . . I hope so."

Branches smacked his cheeks as they sprinted through the thick trees, but this time Jamal didn't care. The dolls chased them, cutting through the underbrush. He could hear the rustling and splashing of their tiny feet. Shadows also reached out as if to snare them in their sharp claws.

Jamal waved the skull necklace around, the reddish light warding off the shadow monsters and protecting them as they fled through the marsh.

Suddenly, he felt something snare his ankle.

He glanced down. It was the one of the dolls.

It had its fingers latched around his leg. Its face, stitched from crude fabric, stared up at him. The button eyes looked empty. It stopped his blood cold.

"Get off me!" Jamal kicked hard, but the doll held on.

Then another doll leapt out of the cypress trees, landing on his shoulders. It scrambled for his neck, reaching toward the skull necklace.

The necklace flared brighter in response.

But the doll wasn't affected by the light like the shadow monsters. The thing snagged the necklace and pulled it, strangling Jamal with the chain. More dolls leapt at him, latching on to his legs, his arms, his torso, his neck. They kept jumping out of the trees at him.

"No, help me—" he yelled.

Smack!

Suddenly, a branch whacked the first doll on his neck, sending it flying.

"Didn't you hear him?" Riley snarled. "He said . . . get off!"

She clutched the branch like a baseball bat, knocking the dolls off him. Then she grabbed his hand, and again they set off, running through the bayou. But the dolls chased them. Their tiny feet rustled the underbrush all around them. The dolls were almost impossibly fast.

"Hurry, this way," Riley called out, pulling Jamal deeper into the swamp. They splashed forward and waded up to their waists in the standing water.

Jamal glanced around for his brother. "Malik, where are you?"

There was no answer. Fear rushed through him like ice water.

Riley glanced back at him. The reddish light from the skull necklace washed over her face. Terror lit up her eyes. "Listen, we have to swim," she hissed. "It's the only way to lose them."

Jamal plunged deeper into the water and swam after her, trying not to think about the poisonous snakes and other creatures lurking all around them. The skull necklace lit their way.

"Watch out, Little J!" Malik rasped behind Jamal.

Suddenly, two red eyes, glowing like embers, lit up in the black water.

Then another set of red eyes.

And another.

"Uh . . . w-what're those?" Jamal stammered, pointing to them.

Then he saw their jaws crack open in the water. They were filled with rows of sharp teeth. They gnashed and snapped at the air hungrily.

"Oh, no . . . gators!" Riley yelped.

"But why're their eyes glowing?" Jamal asked.

"They must be bewitched . . . by the shadow man's friends on the other side. . . ." Riley coughed, sputtering on water. "That tree . . . over there . . . we have to get to it!"

More red eyes opened in the dark water and chased them.

They swam toward a cypress tree that grew out of the middle of the marsh like a little island. But the gators were gaining on them.

Riley reached the tree first and scrambled up the thick

roots. Her hands slipped, but then she hooked a branch. She reached back for Jamal. Their eyes met for a split second.

"My hand—grab it," she yelled.

He swam toward the tree, but the gators were right behind him. He could see their red eyes drawing closer. He held his breath and tried to swim faster.

Desperately, Jamal reached up and clasped her hand. She yanked him up onto the tree right as a gator snapped at his ankle, almost taking his foot off.

They scrambled farther up the roots while the bewitched gators swarmed around the cypress tree, circling it and blocking any means of escape. Their red eyes glowed in the murky water. The sun had fully set, and the swamp was pitch-black.

They were trapped.

"Malik . . . are you here?" Jamal called, feeling panicked that they'd lost him in the chase.

"Right behind you," Malik rasped. "Even though you can't see me."

"At least we're safe up here," Riley said, clinging to the tree. "Gators can't climb trees—"

But then a gator scrambled up the roots.

It snapped at them.

And then the others followed, climbing the tree.

"Wait, gators can't do that," Riley hissed. "How's that possible?"

"These aren't normal gators," Jamal said, snagging her hand and pulling her up higher.

He struggled to hold on, but his hands were wet from swimming and slipped on the slick tree bark. He plummeted down, right toward a gator. It snapped at his leg. He scrambled away but then slipped down farther. The gator opened its jaws, its teeth glinting in the dim light.

Suddenly, a voice boomed out of the darkness.

"Foul creature, release them! Go back to your swamp!"

15

THE DOLLS

A flash of reddish light illuminated the bayou, driving the gators back into the water. They snapped at the air, angry to be denied their prey. Jamal's eyes fell on the source of the light.

On the edge of the swamp stood an old woman with brown skin just like Riley's, clutching a staff hewn from gnarled, twisted cypress wood. A crystal adorned the top of it and glowed red in the darkness.

The old woman threw back the hood of her cloak, revealing hair and eyes that were, oddly, bright blue.

"Grandma!" Riley called.

"Hold tight, child," her grandmother called in her resounding voice. She turned her attention back to the gators, who had regrouped and circled around the cypress tree.

Her grandmother reached into her cloak and pulled out a handful of glittering silver dust. Jamal flinched back when he saw it, recognizing it as similar to the magic the shadow man used.

The old woman blew it at the gators.

"Release these foul creatures from your dark magic," she boomed out, blowing the dust at them. "And return to the shadows—where you belong."

The silver dust clouded the air, swirling around the gators. They slowly stopped circling the tree. Their eyes blinked out, one by one, the reddish light extinguished.

She had broken the spell.

Released from the dark magic, the gators quickly retreated into the bayou, consumed by the murky depths. Riley and Jamal waited until they were sure they were gone, then clambered down the tree and swam to the banks of the swamp.

"Oh, my child, are you hurt?" Grandma DeSeroux said, stooping down to pull Riley into a hug. The crystal on top of her staff glowed. She checked her granddaughter over for injuries.

"Grandma, we're fine," Riley said. "But we wouldn't have been for much longer if you hadn't found us. . . ."

"The shadow man," Grandma DeSeroux said in a sharp voice, her strange blue eyes narrowing when they fell on Jamal. "This is his dark magic. I'd sense it anywhere. I tracked it out here and found you."

"Yup, that's what we thought, too," Riley said with a nod.

"But he rarely ventures into my bayou," Grandma DeSeroux said with a frown that deepened the wrinkles in her brown skin and made her look even older. "He knows better than that. What's drawn him out here?"

"Well, that's why we're here," Riley said. "This is my friend Jamal. Dr. Facilier cursed his brother and turned him into a *shadow*."

"A shadow curse?" Grandma DeSeroux said, raising her eyebrows. "That's not something you want to mess with."

She raised her staff, casting a halo of reddish light that fell over Malik, making his shadow form stand out. Her eyes widened in fear when she saw him; then they shifted to Jamal.

"Oh, no, my child," she said. "I fear that your brother is already fading. We don't have much time. Quickly, follow me!"

* * *

"Children, hurry!" Grandma DeSeroux said in an urgent tone. "This way!"

Riley's grandmother led them through the bayou, using the light from her staff to guide the way. Despite the thick underbrush, roots that threatened to trip them with each step, and marshy earth, she was sure-footed and moved quickly.

Jamal was the one who struggled to keep pace with the old woman. He slipped, then righted himself at the last minute. Mud sloshed up his legs. He followed right behind Riley and her grandmother while Malik stuck to him like a second shadow.

Somehow the swamp feels less scary with her leading the way, he thought.

He glanced from Riley to her grandmother, taking

in their appearances. In spite of their age difference and their haircuts and clothes, he could see the family resemblance. It had something to do with their eyes. Even though Riley's were brown and her grandmother's were that odd blue, there was a sharpness in both. A glint. It was as if they could both really *see* things.

Suddenly, he heard something rustling in the trees behind them.

The skull necklace exploded to life with reddish light, glowing underneath his shirt. His heart thudded faster.

"The dolls!" he said, glancing back into the thick darkness of the bayou.

Riley gasped. "Oh, no, they must be following us."

She reached back and clasped his hand. Her palms were slick with sweat. He felt a jolt when their hands met, but this time it wasn't fear—it was something else altogether. It felt powerful and deep, like something almost magical. *But what does it mean?* he wondered.

"Stubborn little creatures," Grandma DeSeroux muttered, turning around and wielding her staff. "They're not easily deterred—not once they've set their sights on what they most desire."

"Most desire?" Jamal repeated, swallowing hard against his fear.

"My child, you must have something the shadow man greatly desires," she said, leading them deeper into the bayou, "or he wouldn't chase us this far. He knows this is my territory. I fear he must be growing stronger. Usually the protections would keep him away."

The rustling drew closer; then the dolls burst through the trees. Their faces looked horrific—lopsided, with button eyes, stitched mouths, and slits for noses.

Their eyes locked on to Jamal.

Moving with incredible speed, they scrambled from the underbrush toward him. Some scaled the trees, rustling through the branches overhead. Soon they'd spring on him.

He shut his eyes, bracing for the attack, when he heard Grandma DeSeroux's voice.

"Foul creations, begone," Grandma DeSeroux boomed out, producing more silver dust. She blew it at the dolls. The dust clouded the air, obscuring the dolls from their view.

"Children, come fast," Grandma DeSeroux hissed. "That'll throw them off—but not for long."

Then she grabbed Riley's hand, pulling them forward, and extinguished the light from her staff. Darkness enveloped them. *Thick* darkness. *Pure* darkness. Jamal felt himself choking on it. He couldn't see anything. But he held fast to Riley's hand like his life depended on it.

Because in a way, it did.

"Malik, are you with me?" Jamal whispered to the darkness, to the shadows.

Silence.

Had he lost his brother forever?

But then—

"Don't worry, I'm here . . . Little J," rasped Malik. "Right behind you."

Was it Jamal's imagination, or did his voice sound weaker? He remembered Grandma DeSeroux's words: *I fear that your brother is already fading.* He just hoped she could help them.

A few minutes later, Grandma DeSeroux lit up her staff again. The reddish light fell over a rustic hut, surrounded by a trickling stream. It looked simple yet idyllic, but, more important, like a safe place. One word rushed through Jamal's head.

Home.

It looked like home.

"You'll be safe here," Grandma DeSeroux said, throwing open the front door and ushering them inside. "There are ancient protections."

Her hut was more spacious than it appeared from the outside, like an optical illusion. *How is this possible?* Jamal wondered. Inside, a fire flickered, casting warm light over the comfy interior.

Masks of all shapes and sizes adorned the walls, while patterned fabrics covered the furniture and brightened the decor. There was a simple single bed, a lumpy old sofa, and a knobby rocking chair carved from cypress wood. Jamal glanced at the stained glass windows, wondering if the dolls were lurking outside, waiting for them to emerge from the hut. He just hoped her ancient protections would be enough to keep them away.

Grandma DeSeroux cast off her cloak, hung it on a peg, then settled into the rocking chair with a sigh. Jamal noticed that her black hair, braided back from her face, was streaked with gray. She still clutched her staff. Jamal got the feeling that she never set it aside.

Her sharp eyes fixed on them. "Have a seat, my children," she said in her clear voice. "Make yourselves at home. My house is your house."

Riley led Jamal to the sofa, where they settled in. He glanced down, realizing how filthy he was from their trek through the bayou, and immediately felt bad for tarnishing her clean hut. Malik flowed over the floor and took his place by Jamal.

"Oh my, your poor brother," Grandma DeSeroux said, her eyes following Malik as his dark form moved across the floorboards. "Tell me everything, my child. Leave nothing out."

Jamal swallowed hard to still his nerves, then explained everything that had transpired: his grandmother's leaving him her skull necklace when she passed away; Dr. Facilier's coming after him and promising him the future he most desired; Jamal's trading his brother's trumpet to him instead of the necklace, then waking up to a world where he had replaced his brother altogether.

"And then I found out that my brother had become a walking, talking shadow," Jamal finished, casting his eyes down to the creaky old floorboards. "And it's all my fault. I never should have trusted the shadow man."

Grandma DeSeroux shook her head. She rose from her rocking chair and poured them mugs of steaming herbal tea from the pot simmering gently over the fire.

"My child, that's what he does," she said, handing Jamal a mug. The mug was warm—and it did make him feel better. "He preys on folks' deepest, darkest fears, then makes them an offer they can't refuse. He promises them what they most desire. But it's always a trick to get what he really wants. He's fooled more poor souls than I can count."

"But . . . can you help me?" rasped Malik, his voice fading in and out.

Jamal realized that it wasn't his imagination: his brother was growing weaker.

Grandma DeSeroux noticed it, too. She looked worried. "I fear he is beginning to fade from this world. I've seen this sort of dark magic before. Soon your brother will cease to exist altogether. You don't have much time to reverse the curse."

"Grandma, you have to help him," Riley said. "You're our only hope."

"Please, how do we fix it?" Jamal added. "There must be a way to help. I'll do anything."

"Child, I wish it were that easy," Grandma DeSeroux said, lowering her head. It was as if a shadow crossed her face, aging her. "This sort of ancient magic isn't easily undone. It is nearly unbreakable."

Jamal felt a jolt of fear. "What do you mean? It can't be reversed?"

Grandma DeSeroux sipped her tea. "Once payment is rendered, and the friends have sent their minions from the other side," she said in a soft voice, "only Dr. Facilier can reverse the curse."

"You were right," Jamal said, pulling out the skull necklace. "I have something that Dr. Facilier greatly desires. I think he cursed my brother to trick me into giving him this."

Grandma DeSeroux's eyes fixed on the necklace and

widened. "Oh yes, he very much wants that necklace. Your grandmother left it to you?"

"Yes, she did," Jamal said, "along with a note—*Beware of the shadows*. Only, I didn't understand what it meant. But maybe if I give it to him, then he'll save my brother."

"Grandma," Riley said, studying her grandmother's visage, "you recognize that necklace, don't you?"

"Oh yes, I do," she replied.

And then she reached into her dress and pulled out a skull necklace that was identical to the one around Jamal's neck.

16

THE CURSE OF
THE SHADOW MAN

"But . . . how on earth do you have the same necklace?" Jamal said.

He stared at the skull necklace around Grandma DeSeroux's neck. It was the twin of the one fastened around his neck. A thousand questions rushed through his head as he struggled to make sense of the situation.

"Oh, my child," Grandma DeSeroux said with a wry smile, "I knew your grandmother. Let's just say . . . she was like me."

"Wait, she had magic?" Jamal said, feeling even more shocked. He glanced at Riley, then at Malik, who shifted around on the floor, contorting.

"Well . . . that would explain a lot . . ." Malik rasped. "She was kind of strange. Never went outside. Wore those dark veils. Barely talked."

"That's one way to describe us," Grandma DeSeroux chuckled. "We were both part of an ancient order of people with good magic. These days, there aren't many of us left in this world. We're sworn to use our powers for good and to protect our city from harm."

Riley frowned. "So how do you know the shadow man?"

"Once upon a time, this . . . entity you're dealing with belonged to our order and used his powers only for good," Grandma DeSeroux said, sipping her tea with a grimace. "But he became fascinated by dark magic and, eventually, consumed by greed and his quest for wealth and power. That was when he named himself after the legendary mythical shadow man, Dr. Facilier."

"Let me guess," Jamal said, feeling his stomach churn sickly. "That was how he became a shadow man himself— by aligning himself with evil magic?"

"That's right," Grandma DeSeroux said. "We expelled him from our order and tried to strip him of his powers.

But he had grown too strong. He fought back and defeated us. Your grandmother tried to stop him. . . . That's why she . . . why she changed so . . ."

She trailed off as if it pained her to finish her thought.

"Right, my mother said something about that," Jamal said. "Like how she wasn't always afraid of the sunlight and unable to venture outside."

He remembered his grandmother sitting in her rocking chair, the thick curtains drawn against the sun, her body draped head to toe with veils.

"Yes, some dark magic leaves a wound," Grandma DeSeroux said. "One that can't be healed. It damaged her too badly. She was never the same. I'm sorry you didn't know her before that happened. Dr. Facilier did that to your grandmother."

Jamal struggled to absorb all of it. He glanced down at Malik, wishing they could make real eye contact. His brother swirled across the floor.

"Tell me about the necklaces," he said, feeling the outlines of the skull sockets pressing into his palm.

"Many long years ago, we forged them to protect us from the shadow man," Grandma DeSeroux said. "Oh, my child, he is far older than he appears. That's some dark magic indeed. Then each member of my order retreated into the shadows to hide from him."

"Our grandmother . . . became a recluse . . ." Malik rasped. "She never left her house. She wouldn't even open the windows. The curtains were always drawn. She wore veils."

"Yes, and I retreated into the bayou to my family's land," Grandma DeSeroux said, "where I'd be safe from the shadow man's magic. Only I fear that over time, he's grown more powerful than even I realized. I'm guessing that he's also the reason your grandmother died. He came after her for that necklace, and she wouldn't give it to him. Instead, she left it to you."

"He killed my grandmother?" Jamal said with a start.

Grandma DeSeroux set her lips in a line. "My child, I'm afraid it looks that way."

"But if the necklace is supposed to protect me," Jamal said, thinking it over, "and she left it to me to protect me from him, then why could he curse my brother?"

"Dr. Facilier can't curse you directly," she explained,

"and he can't take the necklace unless you give it to him, because of the protection spells placed on it. But because you gave him something of great value to your brother, it rendered him vulnerable to the shadow curse."

"Ugh, I'm so stupid," Jamal said, his head falling into his hands. Remorse washed through him. "I have to fix this. I'm going to give him the necklace so he'll reverse the curse."

"My child, then Dr. Facilier will grow even more powerful," Grandma DeSeroux said with a worried frown. "Eventually he might get more of the necklaces from the remnants of my order. Then there will be nothing and no one to stop him."

"But I have to save my brother and reverse the curse." Jamal jumped to his feet and paced around her hut. "You said yourself that he's already fading. If I don't at least try to make a deal with the shadow man, then my brother will disappear forever. I can't let that happen."

Grandma DeSeroux looked deeply troubled. "It is a terrible choice indeed," she muttered. "But that's how the shadow man works."

"Isn't there something you can do?" Jamal said, looking at her in desperation.

He was used to living in a world where adults held all the power and could always help him. He had expected that Riley's grandmother would save them from the shadow man. But what if the adults didn't have the ability to save them? What if it was up to him this time?

"My child, you have to make a choice," Grandma DeSeroux said. "I wish I could help, but it's up to you to decide now. It's either Malik . . . or the entire city of New Orleans."

"But how do I make that choice?" Jamal asked. "Either way, somebody loses."

"I'm so sorry, my child. I wouldn't wish that sort of terrible choice on anyone. But I know you'll do the right thing—" she started before the door to the hut blew open.

She whipped her head around. Jamal followed her gaze: the dolls crowded into the doorway. Their button eyes fixed on Jamal hungrily. They wanted the necklace.

"W-what . . . they broke my protection spells?" Grandma DeSeroux stammered, clutching her staff and raising it. "Child, the shadow man's power has grown stronger."

The dolls' eyes fixed ravenously on the skull necklace.

Jamal felt a jolt of fear and tucked the necklace away into his shirt. He couldn't let them get it. The necklace was his only bargaining chip to use with Dr. Facilier to save his brother.

The dolls swarmed through the doorway, scrambling across the floor toward Jamal.

"Riley, get your staff!" Grandma DeSeroux yelled, lighting up her own.

Riley grabbed a smaller staff, raising it to fight against the dolls. She reached into her pocket, producing a handful of gold dust. She joined her grandmother.

"Wait, you have good magic, too?" Jamal said in shock, staring at Riley.

"Grandma's been training me," she said, "ever since we moved back. . . . It runs in my family's blood."

Riley blew the dust at the dolls. It swirled around them, but then it faded and the dolls regrouped and lurched toward Jamal. One doll grabbed his foot, while another reached for his arm, and another leapt off the sofa toward his neck.

"Protect the necklace!" Grandma DeSeroux yelled, blowing more dust at them. "Riley and I will hold them off—but you have to run. Take your brother. They're too strong. We can't hold them back forever."

* * *

"Malik, hurry," Jamal yelled as he fled from the hut with his shadow brother trailing right behind him.

He glanced back, hearing sounds of struggle coming from behind them. Unnatural explosions of reddish light and silver and gold dust swirled around the hut as Riley and her grandmother fought back against the dolls. Jamal hoped they would be okay, but he didn't have time to worry.

Run.

Grandma DeSeroux's cries echoed through his head, spurring him to run faster. He staggered into the dark bayou, plunging into murky water that sloshed over his shoes. A warm wind whipped through the cypress trees while thunder rumbled and lightning crackled.

"The hurricane . . ." Malik warned in his ear. "I think it's making landfall tonight. . . . I heard it on the news."

Jamal remembered his parents watching the local news and tracking the new storm. It had recently intensified over the Gulf of Mexico. It was now threatening their city.

More lightning bolts exploded overhead, followed by a sharp crackle of thunder. The bayou lit up for one brilliant second, then fell into thick darkness again.

Hurricanes were a normal part of life in their gulf city. But as Jamal looked up at the sky, he realized that something seemed different about this storm. *Unnatural*, even.

"The shadow man," Malik rasped, as if reading his mind. "I can't explain it . . . but since he cursed me . . . it's like I can feel his magic."

"Are you saying this hurricane is his doing?" Jamal said, his stomach clenching. He ran blindly, water sloshing up to his ankles now.

"Not his doing, exactly," Malik gasped out right behind him. His voice sounded even weaker. "But it's like . . . he made it worse somehow. I can't explain it."

That made Jamal more afraid. He thought about the deal he was considering making with Dr. Facilier—trading the skull necklace for his brother's life. But if what Riley's grandmother said was true, then the necklace would make the shadow man even stronger.

Could he take that risk?

More lightning pulsed overhead, accompanied by a deafening clap of thunder. Meanwhile, the wind was growing stronger, rattling the cypress branches draped with moss. Each time the bayou lit up, the shadows twisted around them, reaching out their clawed hands.

Jamal dodged the shadow monsters, running faster. Then the skull necklace lit up, glowing with reddish light. "Oh, no, he's coming," he hissed, trying to run even faster.

He burst into a clearing when, suddenly, red light exploded over the bayou.

It wasn't lightning this time—it was something else.

A long reedy shadow stretched over the clearing, extending toward them like a curse. The skeletal figure had almost impossibly slender arms and legs, and a top hat perched on his head.

THE CURSE OF THE SHADOW MAN

The shadow clutched a staff. The crystal on it glowed with red light.

It was Dr. Facilier.

Then the shadow man himself stepped into the clearing, behind his shadow. He clutched his staff, with the crystal glowing dark red. He grinned, his teeth resembling an alligator's.

He stood taller than before. He tipped his top hat toward Jamal.

"*Enchanté*, little man," he said in a smooth voice. "A tip of the hat."

Then, suddenly, Dr. Facilier's shadow came to life, uncoupling from him and acting of its own accord.

It flowed across the clearing and pounced on Malik, startling him with clawed fingers. Malik tried to fight back, but he was too weak.

Jamal lurched toward the two shadows to help his brother, but his hands passed through them harmlessly. He couldn't touch them.

"No, leave him alone!" Jamal, feeling helpless, yelled at Dr. Facilier.

The shadow man chuckled, his voice echoing through the bayou and raising all the hair on Jamal's body.

"There's only one way to make it stop," the shadow man said. "Don't waste my time any longer. The necklace—hand it over now. Or say goodbye to your precious brother forever."

17

FIENDS ON THE OTHER SIDE

"The necklace—in exchange for your brother's life," Dr. Facilier demanded, reaching his hand toward Jamal. "No negotiations this time, little man. My offer is final."

Lightning flashed in the sky and thunder crackled. Thick droplets of rain started to pelt them. Meanwhile, Dr. Facilier's shadow twisted Malik's neck, strangling him. Jamal's brother was fading even more.

"Little J . . . help me," Malik rasped weakly.

"Let him go!" Jamal yelled.

He pulled the skull necklace out. The eye sockets glowed with light, warning him not to do it. Grandma

FIENDS ON THE OTHER SIDE

DeSeroux's voice echoed in his head: *Then there will be nothing and no one to stop him.*

But Jamal pushed her voice away. *I have to do this,* he thought in desperation. *I have to save my brother.*

He unclasped the thick chain from his neck. Then he reached out to give Dr. Facilier the skull necklace.

"Don't do it, Jamal!"

Riley burst into the clearing, clutching her staff. "You can't trust him. My grandma told me. He'll just trick you again."

She blew her dust at Dr. Facilier's shadow.

The shadow contorted in pain—and released Malik! Then Riley ran at Dr. Facilier with her staff raised, but before she could get to him, the dolls burst into the clearing.

They seized Riley, overpowering her this time.

"No, let me go!" she yelled, struggling against the dolls, but there were too many of them. They jumped on her and held her down, restraining her.

"Seize the shadow brother," Dr. Facilier said, flicking his wrist. His shadow responded by grabbing Malik. It started to devour him.

"Stop!" Jamal yelled. "They're my friends . . . my only *real* friends."

It was the shadow man's enchantment that had made Colton and the others at school like him. But Riley had liked him before he made that deal with Dr. Facilier, and his brother had always had his back, protecting him from the bullies. They were his *real* friends.

He had to save them.

"Little man, don't waste my time," Dr. Facilier ordered, peering from under the brim of his top hat. "Your grandmother's necklace . . . *now*."

Jamal glanced at the dolls. They were latched on to Riley, holding her down. She struggled against them, but they were too strong. Their button eyes followed the necklace hungrily. Jamal moved his hand right, then left. Anywhere he moved the necklace, their eyes followed it.

Suddenly, he had an idea. "Wait, what happens if you don't get this necklace?" Jamal asked, holding it up over his head. The doll's eyes followed it. "What if I break it?"

Fear flashed over Dr. Facilier's face. The doll's eyes darted to *him* now.

Suddenly, Jamal understood: Dr. Facilier had asked

his friends on the other side for help, and they had sent these *things* to do their bidding, but he had to get the necklace as payment or his "friends"—and the dolls— would turn on him.

"They'll come after you, won't they?" Jamal said. "The dolls. You have to get this for your friends—or else!"

"That's right," Riley yelled from the ground. "If he doesn't provide the necklace, he's doomed. They'll take his soul."

Jamal raised the necklace to smash it.

Dr. Facilier held up his hands, trying to stop him.

"Little man, don't act so hastily," he pleaded. "Let's talk about this. I'm a wheeling, dealing man. I'm sure we can work something out—"

The dolls released Riley and started toward Dr. Facilier. The dolls surrounded him, staring up at him with their button eyes.

"If they take my soul," he snarled at Jamal, "then you'll never get your brother back. I'm the only one who can reverse the shadow curse."

Jamal flinched. This was the terrible choice he had

to make. He remembered what Grandma DeSeroux had said. It was either Malik or the entire city of New Orleans.

"Little J, don't do it," Malik rasped in a strangled voice. The shadow monster had almost fully devoured him now. "I'm not worth it. Save our city. . . . Don't do it!"

Jamal watched him start to disappear and felt his heart lurch painfully. The truth hit him all at once. He couldn't stand to live in a world where his brother didn't exist anymore. They were twins, and Malik was like a part of him.

He lowered his hand.

"Here . . . take the necklace," Jamal said in defeat, holding it out.

Dr. Facilier grinned. His hand closed around the thick chain. Smoothly, he fastened it around his neck. The eye sockets lit up with reddish light—and Dr. Facilier's eyes glowed red, too. He started to grow taller and taller, his form enveloping the bayou.

"Okay, reverse the curse," Jamal said, turning toward his brother.

But Malik remained a shadow. Suddenly, Jamal felt like something strange was happening to him.

He glanced down at his hands, but they had turned dark and transparent . . . like a shadow.

"Wait, what's happening to me?" Jamal screamed, but his voice came out raspy, just like his brother's voice.

He was now a shadow, too.

An evil chuckle echoed through the bayou. Lightning and thunder tore through the turbulent sky while rain poured down from the hurricane.

"Now you know what it's like to really lurk in the shadows," Dr. Facilier said with a tip of his hat. "You should've listened to your grandmother. You can't trust the shadow man."

"But you promised to bring my brother back," Jamal rasped, "not to turn me into a shadow, too."

He felt himself fading even more. Another chuckle rang out.

"Little man, I promised you no such thing," Dr. Facilier said with an evil grin. He grew even bigger, stretching almost as tall as the trees that surrounded them. "You heard what you chose to hear. And now you'll pay the price—and so will the city you love."

The last thing Jamal heard as he faded into a shadow altogether was Dr. Facilier's evil laugh echoing across the bayou.

18

THE SHADOWLANDS

"Carter, turn the volume up," their mother called from the kitchen.

"Sure thing," Dad said, reaching over from stirring the gumbo, and pumping up the volume.

"Aftermath from Hurricane Donald continues to wreak havoc on our city," the reporter spoke into the microphone, showing the swirling pattern of the storm that had passed over the city. It had been a direct hit.

The local news carried footage of the recent damage from the hurricane. Flooded streets. Garbage strewn everywhere. Shattered storefronts. Roofs caved in. Fires from lightning strikes that burned around the city.

The power was still out in the French Quarter, and the streets were dark and shadowy. Some of the shadows even seemed to take on monstrous forms, depending on who you asked.

Only one business seemed strangely unaffected—Dr. Facilier's Voodoo Emporium.

"Is it luck or magic?" the reporter joked with a knowing chuckle.

"Thank god we moved out of the floodplain," their mother said, watching with a frown. "Otherwise we'd be going through it all over again. Maybe losing another home."

"Oh, we're so fortunate," their father agreed. "With climate change, it's only going to get worse. . . ."

Dad carried the pot to the table. Mom took a seat and ladled out heaping helpings of gumbo. The table was set for only two people.

There was no sign of Jamal or Malik.

"The mayor is giving a press conference on the storm," said the reporter, dressed in a yellow rain slicker.

Their parents watched as the image cut away from

the streets. On the television, the mayor stepped up to the podium. He had dark skin, a thin mustache, and a smile with a big gap right in the middle. He wore a purple suit and clutched a staff with a crystal on it. On his head perched a top hat with a skull and crossbones. Around his neck hung a skull necklace. The eye sockets glowed deep red. He tipped his hat forward and leaned into the microphone.

"*Enchanté*, citizens of the great city of New Orleans," he said in his silky smooth voice. He grinned widely. "Due to the damage from the recent storm, I've been forced to seize power and issue a state of emergency. The city is now under martial law. . . ."

It was Dr. Facilier.

Outside, neighborhood kids splashed in the water flowing through the streets. In the gutters they sailed homemade boats, some of which vanished into the storm drains.

Dad glanced outside and frowned. "Kiara, I'm so glad we decided not to have kids. Especially with all these hurricanes. It's a dangerous world we live in."

He reached over and clasped her hand. She smiled at him.

"Me too," she replied, squeezing his hand. "I'm so happy with just the two of us."

"But we're right here!" Jamal cried from the shadows. *"Mom . . . Dad . . . we're your children! Can't you see us?"*

But it was no use. Jamal and Malik were both shadows. Their parents couldn't see or hear them, no matter how hard they tried to get their attention. They both continued shouting at their parents, but still it made no difference. It was like they didn't exist.

In the living room, the family pictures showed only their mother and father. There were no pictures of Jamal or Malik. It was as if they had never existed, thanks to the shadow curse.

"How do we get back from the other side?" Jamal asked his brother.

Malik stared back at him. He was still fading, but it had slowed since Jamal had joined him in the shadows. However, both of them would eventually disappear altogether. They could feel it.

Dr. Facilier's laugh echoed out of the television set,

though their parents seemed oblivious to it. Dr. Facilier's eyes fixed on Jamal's and Malik's shadow forms.

"Now you know what it's like to lurk in the shadows . . . *forever!*"

ACKNOWLEDGMENTS

I want to start by thanking Disney Books and my amazing editor, Kieran Viola, for entrusting me with their villains (and yes, for the record, they do have the best ones). It's a dream come true to write about Disney characters, especially the *creepy* ones. To quote Dr. Facilier, "dreams made real." Special thanks to Kieran for being a fabulous editor and always making my writing stronger. Collaborating with you has been simply fantastic. Looking forward to many more books together. Also, as always, thanks to my book agent, Deborah Schneider, who believed in me from the beginning and always looks out for me and the rest of my team.

I want to thank my special someone. Babes, you were

there with me through the drafting of this book on an extremely tight deadline. You made my life better and helped when I despaired, brainstormed with me, kept me focused, cooked me dinner, always told me I could do it. Love having you in my corner.

Special thanks to my family, especially my parents for introducing me to Disney stories early on and getting me the Disney Channel when I was a kid. You probably worried that I watched way too much, but without those early influences, I wouldn't be half the writer I am today.

Dear readers, special thanks to you. Apologies if this book gave you nightmares or kept you up way past your bedtime. (But those are the best kind of books, aren't they?) I hope your parents will find a way to forgive me. But reading is *everything*. It's a ticket to brave new worlds and special friends and fantastical places. It will open up your mind and your life.

Don't ever stop. You will never regret reading a book. Thank you for choosing mine. It means everything.

You are why I write.

—Jennifer Brody